MISCHIEF AT FRINTON PARK

A rainy day in October of the year 1812, and the young people, idling away their time in the Morning Room at Frinton Park, are bored. Boredom breeds mischief, and it is not long before a cruel practical joke is hatched in the fertile minds of Francis, George and Sarah, the Darker triplets.

A simple switching of identities and Francis, who has military ambitions, carelessly abandons the girl who loves him and goes off to war. Unaware that she has been betrayed, the fetching Lucy Briggs-Watson marries George Darker in the belief that he is Francis, but the marriage is not a success.

When Miss Emily Pinkerton, George's mistress, uncovers the truth she seizes the opportunity to make her lover pay for her silence. With their backs to the wall, George and Sarah Darker are forced to resort to desperate measures in order to extricate themselves from a situation which is rapidly getting out of control.

By the same author

John Plantagenet
The Coveted Crown
The Lion and the Lily
The Passionate Prince
The Spanish Tudor
Bess
The People's Martyr
Lords of the Manor
The bartered Queens
The Queen's Progress
The Brandon Brood
Three Crowns For Mary
Royal Clown
The Gilded Cage
The Murder of Caroline Matilda
Requiem For Richard
The Hundred Days
An Admirable Woman
For the Love of Albert
The Master of Frinton Park
The Heir of Frinton Park

MISCHIEF AT FRINTON PARK

by

FREDA M. LONG

ROBERT HALE · LONDON

First published in Great Britain 1978

ISBN 0 7091 6751 2

Robert Hale Limited
Clerkenwell House
Clerkenwell Green
London EC1R 0HT

Printed and bound in Great Britain by
A. Wheaton & Co. Ltd, Exeter

OCTOBER, 1812

A Conspiracy to Deceive

An atmosphere of impenetratable gloom pervaded the Morning Room of Frinton Park, where three young persons sat listlessly contemplating the dreary prospect of yet another day to be spent within doors. Outside the heavens opened, sending forth a deluge such as Noah must have witnessed upon the bowed crowns of sturdy elm and beech, and creating a miniature lake in the valley which separated the park from the wilderness beyond. Riding or walking were out of the question; only interminable games of chess and backgammon offered hope of diversion.

Francis Darker, the eldest of the three—he was ten minutes older than his sister Sarah and twenty-five minutes older than his brother George—suggested without much enthusiasm, "We could go upstairs and bait Grandpapa into rattling away. He can be quite diverting on the subject of the slave-trade."

"Old men's tales!" scoffed Sarah, clicking away industriously with an ivory cup and ball. Her next words were punctuated by little exhalations of effort as she endeavoured to keep the game going without breaking rhythm. "He will begin by trying to . . . shock us . . . regaling our innocent young ears with details . . . *puff, click* . . . of all the black females he has sold to his friends for doxies. Then . . . he will go on about supplying silver collar boys to Queen Charlotte . . . a hundred at least . . . *puff, click* . . . after which he will bring his discourse to a conclusion by roundly cursing Mr Wilberforce and his cronies in Parliament for spoiling all his fun."

The others laughed. Francis said with a chuckle, "Do you remember the day we heard that Parliament had passed a Bill abolishing the traffic in blacks? Grandpapa went roaring about the house, with a bottle of smuggled Geneva in one hand and a glass in the other, and we all hid in the linen-closet until Papa got him to bed."

Sarah doubled up with laughter. "Poor Papa. He is never much given to profanity, but he surpassed himself that day."

"And Mama fetched up with a headache," remembered George, a touch of irony creeping into his voice. Mama's headaches were in the habit of appearing quite spontaneously at times of family crisis. Reverting to his sister's previous remarks concerning old William Darker's tendency towards exaggeration, he observed mildly, "I believe Grandpapa's stories have a great deal of truth in them. Some quite dreadful things did happen years ago."

"Some quite dreadful things are happening now," put in Francis, with an indulgent grin for his brother's earnestness. "On the sugar plantations in the West Indian Islands blacks are beaten to death every day. We can properly forget all that, of course. The West Indies are thousands of miles away, and the smell is not under our noses."

Deftly, and with a last triumphant yelp, Sarah captured the ball in the cup. "There!" she exclaimed, "that is fifty times without missing." Quite smoothly, but with disconcerting suddenness she progressed to the attack. "I did not know that you had joined the ranks of the Evangelicals, Francis. If you feel an attack of piety coming on perhaps you had better give up your visits to that flash-house in Brighton."

This unexpected broadside caused a raising of male eyebrows. It was not like Sarah to show her claws to the two beings she loved best in all the world, and with whom she shared her innermost thoughts. The remark was unjust anyway. Francis, though not indifferent to the charms of a lady of pleasure who inhabited attic lodgings in the Steine at Brighton, avoided the flash-houses in "Bath Bun" Gate like the plague. Some of the prostitutes there were not above twelve years old, poor, starved creatures, owned body and soul by the elegantly attired Madams who kept their own carriages and dwelt in the newly-erected houses in South Parade.

Francis did not repudiate his sister's accusation, for he knew it had its origin in boredom. Instead, he announced emphatically, "We have been cooped up in the house too long. If the rain does not stop by this afternoon I shall have "Sultan" saddled and ride over to Great-Aunt Sophie's house. She has promised me the pick of the stallions she bought at the Lewes horse fair. I believe one of them is a Palomino. I should very much like to try him over Ditchley Down."

"It is quite obvious to me," Sarah said, made sharper-tongued than ever by this proof of Briggs-Watson bounty, "that you are become *quite* the favourite in that particular quarter. Could it have anything to do with your having agreed, albeit reluctantly, to marry Aunt Sophie's feather-brained grand-daughter?"

George, piqued by this reference to Cousin Lucy Briggs-Watson's stupidity, and now faintly alarmed by ominous signs of a breach in the solid wall of Darker family unity, said anxiously, "Perhaps we could try out Mr Schubert's new pieces? I have not looked at the music sheets since they came down from London, and it would be gratifying if I could perfect the violin part before Christmas. According to the editor of "Blackwood's" magazine, Mr Schubert is only fifteen years old. It is truly remarkable, is it not, that one so young should be able to compose such beautiful music? I particularly admire his songs."

The ruse, though plainly apparent, was successful, partly because Sarah was indeed too bored to continue with her verbal pin-pricks, and partly because George, once launched upon a "musical" discussion, could become quite fatiguingly loquacious. His sister yawned immoderately, placing her jaw in imminent danger of dislocation, and put aside the cup and ball. "No music for us today, if you please, George. Mama has one of her headaches. I think Papa mentioned something about extravagance in the choosing of material for three new gowns, and she has taken umbrage. She is presently recumbent in her bed-chamber, with vinegar applied to her forehead and a smelling-bottle to her nose, and will not emerge until supper-time. You may have remarked that her head is never so bad that she cannot eat."

Sarah yawned again, stretching her arms above her head, fists clenched as she tensed her arm muscles preparatory to releasing them with a long, slow sigh. "I too shall repair to my room, in order to bury myself in "The Mysteries of Udolpho"." She gave a mock shiver. "Mrs Radcliff makes my flesh positively creep and my blood run cold. She has the trick of breaking off a narrative just when it is upon the point of becoming most interesting. She extinguishes a lamp at the very moment when a parchment containing some hideous secret is about to be read, or closes a door upon a half-seen intruder. Shadowy forms and half-heard sounds of woe abound in the middle of the night. . . . Oh, it is so truly *thrilling!*"

Francis, disappointingly oblivious to this spine-tingling recital, sat with a heavily brooding expression on his normally good-humoured face. He said morosely, "Lucy is not completely devoid of wit and candour, and she *is* exceedingly handsome."

Two pairs of eyes regarded him with surprise, and Sarah was suddenly ashamed of her own malice. George blushed fiercely and blurted, "Lucy is the handsomest girl in the county."

"Mmm," agreed Francis glumly, and fiddled with the buttons of his waistcoat.

Sarah, who had guessed months ago that George was in love with Lucy Briggs-Watson, sprang to the defence of both her brothers. "Really, I do think it monstrous unfair that you, Francis, who desire nothing better than to buy a commission in the army and join the Earl of Wellington's troops in Portugal, must stay at home and marry a girl you care so little for, simply because you had the ill fortune to be born a few minutes before George, who adores silly little Lucy and would gladly cut off his right arm if by so doing he could marry her!"

An embarrassed silence followed this outburst. It had lain deep beneath the surface for months, this never-to-be-referred-to infatuation which George felt towards Lucy. Now it was out in the open, and one did not know whether to be pleased or to hide one's head in shame. The two young men, more phlegmatic in their approach to life than the mercurial Sarah, were smiling at her a little uncertainly. The fact that they did not take her seriously fed her indignation and turned it to anger. She demanded petulantly, "Why do you not fight for what you want? You are like as two peas in a pod. If you changed places no one would be any the wiser, and you could both achieve your hearts' desire. George could marry Lucy, and Papa could buy Francis a commission in the infantry, or the cavalry, whichever suited him best."

Made breathless by her own outrageous suggestion Sarah fell silent then broke into a series of nervous giggles. "Come now, is it not a fact that Mama can never tell you apart if you dress alike? Have you not done so in the past in order to tease her?"

Her brothers were on their feet now and laughing at her. The tension of the last few minutes was broken. "What a wicked suggestion, Sal!" grinned Francis, and seizing his sister by the hand he ran with her to the large oval mirror which hung on the wall between the tall curtained windows. George followed, and all three stood before their own reflections, staring, as if for the first time, at lineaments which nineteen years had rendered so familiar as to preclude the possibility of objective analysis.

Three pairs of blue eyes, so pale as to be almost opaque,

held identical expressions of solemn appraisal; three frankly arrogant noses were aligned in exact juxtaposition—Sarah was the same height as her brothers—three wide mouths, the upper lips slightly too short to conceal the white, even teeth might have been cast from the same mould. Pale, silver-blonde hair, inherited from heaven knows where, framed these pleasant, youthful faces in which there lurked all the eager anticipation of those who are sure that life can hold only good things in store.

Sarah was the first to move. She backed away from her brothers and placing a hand on each muscular arm pushed them together. Peering between their shoulders she pronounced judgement. "I think it entirely possible that you might practise a quiet deception and never be discovered in it." Thoughtfully she added, "Of course, there are complications which will require a great deal of discussion. Francis must agree to give up his inheritance to George, and be entirely certain that he never intends to re-claim it, and a solemn pact must be made between we three . . . sealed with our blood if necessary . . . never to reveal our secret to a living soul."

Francis and George exchanged startled glances, their previous incredulous amusement dispelled by the sudden, awesome possibilites being opened up by their sister's daring proposal. George was the first to turn away, shoulders heaving erratically, as if to shrug off a distasteful restraint. "No, no," he murmured, "it will not do," and then, with more than a hint of irritation, "What an excessively foolish creature you are, Sarah." His eyes dropped before her unwavering, boldly challenging stare.

Sarah was toying with the tiny pink rosebuds marking the high waist-line of her white muslin dress. "But you wish it *were* possible, do you not, dear George?"

George turned his back on her for answer and went to stand by the centre window. The rain had eased a little. A solitary, adventurous duck braved an untimely end by disporting herself in a large puddle of water which had formed beside the carriage-stand, sending up a shower of droplets as she fluffed out her feathers. George rapped with his knuckles on the window, but if the duck heard she was too absorbed in her preening to take heed of the very necessary warning. George made a mental note to scold the kitchen boys for not marking the whereabouts of their charges more carefully. A duck mangled by carriage wheels was of little use for the table.

Narcissus-like, Francis was still engaging the wide-eyed stare of his own mirror-image. He seemed as if turned to stone. "It could be," he whispered, addressing himself. "*It just could be*."

George, who overheard this low-voiced declaration, replied in a loud, commanding tone, "May I suggest that we all sit down, gather up our scattered wits, and admit that we have taken temporary leave of our senses?"

"By all means let us sit down," Francis agreed, and there was a peculiar, lazy quality about his delivery of these words which the others were quick to notice. Invariably it signified intense excitement. Sarah and Francis took up positions on the scroll-backed sofa, with its faded rose-pink and silver upholstery, while George placed himself directly in front of them upon a matching chair. It was an unconscious ranging of those "for" the motion aligning themselves against he who was "against".

It was Sarah who began the debate. "Should you not like to marry Lucy, George?"

George hesitated before the interested, decidedly mocking glances of his brother and sister, momentarily disliking them for their stubborn insistence that he "own up". At length he blurted, "Indeed, I should, but I should think myself unworthy to be called a gentleman were I to practise such a deception upon her." He added quickly, "Now, pray let us face facts. The whole thing is preposterous, and the sooner we forget about it the better."

Total silence greeted this statement. A minute or two later Sarah said, "So you are willing to sacrifice your only hope of happiness for the sake of your notions of what is to be expected of a gentleman?" Once having conceived an idea Sarah clung to it with the tenacity of a bull terrier. She waxed sarcastic. "When you are fighting in Portugal, a thing which I know you will most heartily detest, I hope it will give you comfort to remember that you have behaved like a *gentleman.*"

Francis joined in the argument. "I do not love Lucy, and have no doubt that I shall make a wretchedly inadequate spouse for the poor girl. My mistress in Brighton will still exercise the prior claim on my attention after we are married."

This was a calculated attempt to provoke George, who rose obligingly to take the bait. "You will have *me* to reckon with if you are unkind to Lucy!"

"But you will be with your regiment in Portugal, will you not, George?" inquired Sarah with deceptive innocence.

At this George looked thoroughly miserable, whereupon Sarah seized her chance. "Why do we not essay a little trial?" She was sweetly persuasive. "George shall take Lucy to the next ball or rout to be held in Brighton, donning your clothes, Francis, and you in turn must make an assignation for the same night with George's milliner friend in North Street. I am sure that George will gladly concede her to your tender care in exchange for his beloved Lucy. If both of you are able to carry it off and remain undetected, we will speak of the matter again. If not, the idea shall be instantly discarded."

"An excellent proposition," approved Francis. "Let us regard the whole thing as a harmless practical joke."

"If Lucy guesses the truth I doubt very much if she will think it either harmless or funny," George said grimly, but he was backing down, and the others knew it.

Sarah's eyes gleamed. "We can make a start tonight with Mama and Papa. Having exchanged clothes, you, my dear brothers, shall come down to supper and attempt an impersonation of each other. Francis, who is habitually talkative, must remain quiet and withdrawn, while George must positively sparkle with wit and good humour. It will be a most interesting experiment."

"And like to fail most miserably," prophesised George, "since I am not well practised at "sparkling" in company."

"A harmless practical joke," repeated Francis, and dared his brother with a look to refuse to take part, but George was still stubbornly determined that the mad scheme should fail, so convincing his brother and sister that he was the only member of the trio who could lay claim to perfect sanity. "I shall play my part in your nonsensical charade," said he grudgingly, "but if Mama and Papa smoke out the truth the joke is to go no further."

"Agreed," answered Francis promptly.

"If I do take Lucy to the next rout," pursued George, speaking, it seemed, almost against his will, "you must instruct me in my part, Francis. What matters are touched upon in conversation between you, what secrets, what . . ." he grimaced, ". . . intimacies take place."

Francis threw him a pitying look. "Your part will be quickly learned, brother. Our conversation is limited to a discussion of the weather, or perhaps, if we are very daring, we may move on to admiring Miss Lucy's gown. As to secrets, there are none, and no intimacies, as you so quaintly put it, have ever taken place between us, save a touch of hands, my arm about her waist in the cotillion, or my hand on her elbow as I lead her to her carriage." He paused for a moment, plainly reflecting on the aridity of a loveless wooing. "Poor Cousin Lucy. She deserves to be happy if it is within the power of any man to make her so." The finality of Francis's tone ignited the first spark of enthusiasm in his brother. Desperate cases required desperate remedies.

Sarah said forlornly, "I wish that I could change places with someone. Then I should not have to marry that odious Dodgson Oliver."

"I think Dodgson is quite an agreeable fellow," George countered mildly.

Sarah ignored him and grumbled on, "Just because his father and Papa made the Grand Tour together."

"Lord Frederick saved father's life while they were on the Grand Tour." George again, in his usual role of counsel for the defence.

"Pooh!" Sarah dismissed the claim with a snap of her fingers. "Papa is as bad as Grandpapa when it comes to old men's tales. Well, at least you two will have your chances," she went on heroically. "For my part, I suppose I must suffer the lot of all women and try to do my duty in silence."

"You may suffer, Sal," grinned Francis, "but it will not be in silence."

"We shall probably all have to suffer if it comes to that," George said. "When we sit down to supper Mama and Papa are bound to spot our deception at once, and the whole silly scheme will have to be abandoned."

Later that evening, however, Mama and Papa appeared to notice nothing amiss. Mama remarked laughingly that George must be practising for evenings in the army mess, since he, who never touched claret, had drunk two full glasses. Had he acquired a taste for it? He believed he might have? Well, that was something to be thankful for. A *gentleman* always enjoyed his claret.

Conversations at Breakfast-time

On the day of the Castle Inn Assembly Ball, about a week after the triplets' momentous discussion in the Morning Room, the family gathered together for breakfast in varying degrees of mood and temper. James Darker, nearly forty-three years old, and already beginning to regret the going out of fashion of wigs, since his fair hair was receding in leaps and bounds from his high, sloping forehead, regarded with some anxiety the pile of letters adorning the silver salver which one of the servants had placed on the sideboard. An inedible dish, it waited like an unspoken threat beside the grilled mutton chops and crisp pink curls of bacon.

James would have preferred to soak up the contents of the weekly post on a full stomach, but the possibility that the rich variety of coloured seals concealed bills for which he was not mentally prepared, prompted him to take up the salver and place it gingerly beside his plate. The blank oval of porcelain, rimmed with gold and decorated with yellow roses, seemed to mock his hollow stomach, for the former still lacked its comforting array of chops, fried potatoes, grilled bacon and coddled eggs, without which rich gastronomic delights a man could not be expected to commence his day's work. James stared at the empty plate for a moment longer, as though expecting the chops and bacon to manifest themselves without the prior intervention of the parlour-maid, who stood by the sideboard waiting for the signal to begin serving.

James Darker was a man with cares. This year's harvest had been poor, due to almost unceasing wet weather from the end of June onwards, and the barley crop, part of which had rotted in the fields, was down to three hundred and thirty bushels, a drop of one hundred bushels on last year's yield. The quality of the barley was poor too, pinched out and not good for malting. Arthur Mulliner, the biggest maltster in Lewes, and a connection by marriage of the Darker family, would be looking elsewhere for someone to supply the deficiency in his needs, always a bad thing, because another ambitious farmer might undercut the Darker reserve figure at the Lewes auction. Next year it would not even be worth putting up the crop to be bid for. New outlets would have to be found, and that took time and a fistful of bribes.

Since the collapse of the slave-trade the Darker family

fortunes had steeply declined. Old William Darker had had most of his capital invested in his three slavers, and when the crash had come there was only the farm to fall back on. True, it was an extensive farm, with a good annual yield in wheat, oats and barley—if the weather was kind—and a fair profit to be made out of sheep, but with the slavers rotting away in Rotherhithe docks, and no blacks to work the farm in return for their keep, the purse-strings had had to be tightened. No doubt the wheel of fortune would turn full circle, and other profitable enterprises suggest themselves for exploitation, but in the meantime certain economies would have to be made.

James frequently admitted to a sense of relief that he had only one daughter for whom he must provide a dowry. Fortunately for him, his sisters, all five of them, had been dowered and married off before Parliament had passed its pious Bill, so there were no single females dependent upon his bounty. As a very young man, imbued with the usual idealistic notions concerning human rights, James Darker had abhorred the buying and selling of slaves, as had his mother before him, but time and a degree of adversity, which had also begun to colour his personal relations with Claudine, his wife, had changed all that, and he now felt that he could have swallowed his scruples in order that he and his family might live together in the luxurious style which only considerable wealth could achieve.

In his battle against rising prices and fading incomes James had not been helped by his wife, who continually ignored his repeated pleas not to run up accounts in the Brighton Emporia. Bills for bonnets, muffs, shoes, parasols and a variety of other feminine gee-gaws winged their way with depressing regularity to the doors of Frinton Park and would, he knew, continue to do so, despite all his protests that such extravagances could not possibly be afforded. Short of keeping his wife locked within doors James saw no remedy which he could usefully apply to the situation. Claudine Darker would go on spending his money as though it sprang from a bottomless coffer until the last penny was gone.

Even James's attempts to enter Parliament, through the good offices of his friend, Lord Frederick Oliver, a charming, red-haired dilettante, had met with failure. Lord Frederick had bought him votes by the dozen, but all his efforts at bribery had foundered when it became known that His Royal Highness, the Prince Regent, wanted the Brighton seat for one of his less affluent friends. The next election was not for another three years; thirty-six months must pass before important contacts could be made and enterprises dreamed up in the thick atmosphere of intrigue and chicanery prevailing in the London clubs.

Claudine Darker took her place beside her husband at the breakfast table, observing out of the corner of her eye as she did so the pile of letters. She offered up a prayer that a bill from a certain Brighton hat shop was not among them. After the recent furore about the dresses it would be too much to expect James to be complacent about five guineas expended on a truly delectable bonnet which had chanced to catch her eye as she strolled by the most expensive establishment East Street could boast. The mere thought of the bill, lurking amidst all that paper, biding its time to spring out and trap her, caused a sharp stab of pain behind her eyelids.

Claudine's headaches were not, as her family firmly believed, invented to save her from the harsher facts of life. They were real, agonisingly real, and they were brought on by the smallest hint of an impending "scene". If Claudine occasionally used a headache as an excuse to escape from an irritating situation, she was doing no more than almost every woman has done since time immemorial.

Claudine was half French. Her father, Dr. Robert Westlake, had once been the Darker family's physician. Having gone to Holland after a scandal in which William Darker had slyly involved him, the physician had changed his name to Hollins and had married a French wife, a handsome if rather dull and undemanding woman, who obeyed his every command. By one of those strange quirks of fate, coincidence, call it what you will, young James Darker, on the homeward leg of his Grand Tour, and accompanied by his friend, Lord Frederick Oliver, had entered the small Dutch village of Cleves on the German border. At the time James had been in a dangerously sick condition which had necessitated the immediate summoning of a physician. That physician had been Robert Westlake, of whose connection with his father James had had no previous knowledge. Once made aware of the identity of his patient the good doctor, after marvelling at the smallness of this world, had set to work to cure the high fever which held James in its grip, and having successfully accomplished this near-miracle, might have been expected to part company with the young man after pocketing a substantial fee. The opportunity thus presented to avenge past hurts, however, had been too great to be resisted, and Dr. Westlake had devised a subtle plan whereby old scores might be settled. It had pleased him to encourage a ripening friendship between James Darker and his only child, Claudine, until friendship had blossomed into love and love into wedded bliss. Robert Westlake had smiled secretly to himself, and for the first time in years his tortured heart had been at peace. Vengeance was sweet indeed.

For his part, William Darker, more than a little preoccupied with a new wife, had accepted fatalistically a *fait accompli* which he had no power to rescind, and had tried to forget that his only son's wife was the daughter of a man he had greatly wronged. They had rubbed along well enough together, William and Claudine, and the latter's parents having shown little inclination to visit England, no embarrassing reunions had taken place.

From time to time Claudine and James had visited Holland, the former returning with horrid little china souvenirs lurking in the darkest recesses of her valises. She insisted upon displaying them to great disadvantage in the Morning Room. The souvenirs had occasioned Claudine's only really serious quarrel with her father-in-law, who, being a man of exceedingly sound judgement and taste in the selection of paintings and *objets d'art*, had flatly refused to allow china dogs and cats, the ubiquity of which gave him nightmares, either into his beautiful upstairs Saloon, or into his Eating Room. As for the Music Room, the creation of his first wife Clarissa, it would be sacrilege to put such bastard objects in there. The Morning Room was different. It was a family room, much used, much abused, and a fit dumping ground for those awful bits of china. It was what came, William confided to himself darkly, when one's son married a woman of humble origin, with a saw-bones for a father and a common baker's daughter for a mother.

These days old William, once more a widower, never showed his face at the breakfast table, taking a light repast in his bedroom and showering the bed-clothes with crumbs and bits of scrambled egg, much to the despair of the upstairs maids. Claudine was grateful for his absence, because William stubbornly refused to have a set of false china teeth made for his deprived mouth which boasted just two teeth. These incisors, set side by side in his upper jaw, gave him the appearance of a rather seedy and very ancient buck rabbit. They also made a horrid rattling whistle when he chewed his food, often driving Claudine from the table with a whispered, "Excuse me . . . one of my headaches."

The triplets, already seated primly at table before the advent of their parents, were equally interested in the pile of letters. One never knew when some exciting piece of news might be revealed after the cracking of a seal. Relatives in London often wrote to announce their imminent arrival on a family visit, or Aunt Augusta, Papa's sister, and according to Papa "a political female if ever I saw one," might write giving vivid details of some delicious morsel of scandal among the great. They all remembered with glee the shocking tales about the wicked Lord Byron and Lady Caroline Lamb. Perhaps another chapter of that absorbing saga would be opened up before their wondering eyes. The odious pair had stunned even the most sophisticated members of London society with their goings-on.

Francis and George had, for the time being, resumed their true identities, much to the disgust of Sarah, who declared rather vulgarly that they would never "pull it off" if they did not practice all the time. Uncertain as yet of their future intentions, however, the brothers chose to ignore her, promising only to go through with the tests upon the unsuspecting Lucy and the equally unsuspecting Brighton milliner, a certain Miss Emily Pinkerton, whose favours George had been enjoying for some time.

Morning greetings having been exchanged, Claudine signed to the parlour-maid to begin serving the food. Alice Futcher was a sloppy girl from Piddingfold Village, the daughter of a thatcher. It was quite remarkable the number of times she managed to deposit a piece of food in one's lap. Claudine had often resolved to give Alice her wages and turn her out of doors, but always the thought of tears and pleadings had produced an incipient headache, and she kept deferring the business "until I feel really *robust*." James, who regarded the dismissal of a female servant as strictly within the province of the mistress of the house, refused to intervene, except to say mildly on occasion, "Have you thought any more about getting rid of Alice, my dear?"—this when an especially hot potato had scorched his knee—to which the unfailing response was, "As soon as I feel really *robust*, James."

The exciting crackle of paper prevented the starting up of a conversation, for if Papa chose to read anything out it was a treat not to be missed by the exchange of an idle word. The expectant company were quickly rewarded for their forbearance, a surprised exclamation turning all heads in James's direction. He did not keep his family in suspense. "This letter," he announced, flourishing a large foolscap sheet, "is from Colonel Douglas Grant. He has offered George a commission in his own regiment of the 48th Foot for the sum of One thousand two hundred and fifty pounds, and the regiment is to sail for Lisbon on the twelfth of November."

James looked thoughtful. "Let me see now, that is five . . . no, six weeks from now. It gives us plenty of time in which to purchase uniform and accoutrements. We must go to London, of course. Messrs. Charles Horton of Piccadilly are the suppliers for most of the superior regiments I believe. I very much fear, my dear George, that you will be gone from these shores before Francis and Lucy are married, but that cannot be helped. It may be that you will return home a seasoned warrior in time to play god-father to their first-born."

George had gone very quiet during this recital. He had put aside his knife and fork and was toying with his blue and gold coffee cup, turning it round and round on the saucer. Francis engaged his brother's eye and said brightly, "That is quite splendid, George. My dear fellow, how I envy you. I would give anything to go in your place."

At this Claudine's fine dark eyes narrowed ominously. She was well aware of her eldest son's burning desire to join the army and was not a little fearful that he might, acting upon a sudden youthful and irresponsible impulse, leave home before the announcement of his wedding to Lucy Briggs-Watson could be made. It was necessary on occasion to remind him of his duty. She did so now with a sharpness contrary to her nature. "That is the most ungallant thing to say, Francis. You could not declare more plainly your light regard for dear Lucy."

Claudine's small mouth, primly pursed in that strange way that many Frenchwomen have, as if to accommodate their tongues in a position best suited to the exigencies of their language, moved discreetly as she dealt with a piece of mutton. "You are fortunate to be marrying such a handsome girl, and her father has been most generous over the matter of her dowry. It is to be paid in a lump sum, so Papa will not be put to the trouble of keeping account of the instalments and reckoning up the interest due. Upon that point you may think yourself very fortunate indeed, for I frequently hear complaints among the county people of dowry instalments falling into arrear and of the embarrassment of having to send out a reminder to one's own relatives by marriage."

"*Je n'aime pas Lucy*," returned Francis stubbornly, with an accent so execrable that he made his mother wince.

"Then you must try a little harder," she insisted. A gentle, sentimental smile hovered about her lips. "I am bound to admit that your dear Papa and I were singularly fortunate in that respect. We fell in love from the very first moment we met."

At this James looked up from his correspondence, smiled back at his wife vaguely and went on reading. But it did not last, our love, *ma cherie*, he silently adjured her, and you are the only one not to realise it. Even our children are aware of the gulf opening up between us. Looking back, James came to the conclusion that his love for Claudine had taken something of a knock soon after her father's connection with the Darker family had been made known to him by William. His own father's revelation had left him uncomfortably aware that he had been the victim of another's desire for revenge. With the knowledge had been born a vague resentment against that other innocent party, his wife.

Aloud James said, "Francis and Lucy will settle down in time and twine together like the oak and the ivy. Just wait until your first-born is placed in your arms, Francis. I'll wager it will make you the proudest man in the whole world."

"You had three first-borns to hold, Papa," Sarah put in mischievously. "Were you proud of us?"

James grinned indulgently at his daughter. "I was when I recovered from the shock. It took two glasses of your Grandpapa's best brandy to revive me."

Sarah, by her remark, had captured her mother's attention. The maternal eye was steady and reproving. "After Francis and Lucy are married we shall set a date for your wedding, my dear Sarah. Mr Oliver will not wait for ever. A kind and complacent young gentleman he may be, but there must be a limit to his patience. There will come a time when he will grow tired of your silly coquetting with army officers at the Castle Inn routs, and there is some danger that he will decide that a plainer, more docile bride will suit him better."

Sarah was visibly taken aback. It was the first time Claudine had rebuked her for indelicate behaviour. Had her guilty secret been uncovered? Flushing slightly she defended herself with a lie. "I have never been 'particular' with any gentleman save Mr Oliver."

"But you have danced with other gentlemen a great deal, your tongue on the wag all the time," countered her mother unbendingly. An infinitessimal pause ensued before Claudine administered the *coup de grâce*. "You must now put Captain Millars quite out of your mind for ever. If he is present at the rout tonight you will say nothing except to wish him good-evening, and you may *not* dance with him. I have been very tolerant with you so far, Sarah, but you must not think that I am blind. I have seen Mr Oliver's downcast looks when you have been dancing with Captain Millars, and frankly I am astonished that he has not spoken to you about your light behaviour before now. Since he has not, I am bound to do so. From now on you must regard yourself as the *property* of Mr Oliver, and you will do him the courtesy of offering him your undivided attention."

Sarah struggled with her tears and the lump in her throat. "It is not *fair!*" she gulped. "Francis and I must both marry where we do not love."

Claudine came back sharply with, "Do you imagine, you foolish creature, that Papa and I would give our consent to your marrying a penniless soldier, who is more interested in your fortune than in your face?"

"Captain Millars does not hold money in high esteem," blurted Sarah indiscreetly. "He said he would marry me in my stockinged feet!"

It took about half a minute for this remarkable confession to penetrate her father's fog of preoccupation as he broke open the seal of a pale pink missive marked "For the Personal and Immediate Attention of Mr James Darker." When it did he looked up quickly, with an air of startled indignation, to demand, "Has the fellow dared to propose?"—and as Sarah hung her head—"Answer me, miss, or would you prefer that I go myself to see Captain Millars?"

Sarah was weeping in earnest now, while Francis and George stolidly waded through their food and tried to look calmly detached. "Y . . . yes, he has," Sarah admitted at last with a little moan of distress, "and I wish very much that I might accept his proposal!"

It was at this juncture that James cleverly split his mind into two parts. One part read the pink missive while the other admonished his daughter. "You are never to speak to Captain Millars again, not even to say good-evening,"—this with a glance at his wife who nodded emphatic agreement—"and in the circumstances I think it prudent to request Lord Frederick to give his approval to a marriage at Christmas . . . God in heaven, what is this?" His yelp of wrath drew a frightened look from Claudine. "Five guineas for a hat! What is it made of, *solid gold!*"

Claudine's head immediately began to throb. She had stirred up a hornet's nest with Sarah, and now James was at her about a silly quizz of a hat which she was not quite sure suited her anyway. She rose abruptly from the table, throwing aside her napkin as she did so. "My head," she whispered. "I must go and lie down." Before James could object she was gone, with a swirl of apple-green organza and a backward glance of appeal at her husband.

Sarah sat staring miserably at her unfinished food while a grim determination slowly took possession of her. Whatever the cost in terms of self-sacrifice she would do her utmost to free Francis and George from the shackles of hide-bound convention.

The ruin of a reputation

The Castle Inn Assembly Rooms, designed by the architect John Crunden, were contained in a tall building of rosy red brick pierced by slender arched windows. Inside this pleasant looking edifice were four main rooms, the most important of which was the ballroom. A perfect double cube, eighty feet long and forty feet high and wide, the ballroom had been designed with recesses at each end framed by columns of a most distinguished form—similar to some that the famous Robert Adam had frequently used—with capitals like a plain inverted bell. The walls of this imposing chamber were decorated with plaster reliefs in panels and medallions, and above the frieze at each end were paintings of Dawn and Night; the ceiling was constructed in the form of a shallow arched vault.

On this rather mild night in mid-October the ballroom, the windows of which afforded a splendid view of the Prince Regent's fabulous oriental pavilion, was stiflingly hot. Lit by five hundred candles placed in ornate crystal-drop chandeliers, and heated by two log fires, the heavy atmosphere catered almost exclusively to the comfort of the thinly-clad ladies in their high-waisted organdie and muslin dresses—delicate fabrics which revealed more then they concealed, and probably accounted for the reputation for licentiousness which clung to the Regency period like limpets along the cliff wall at Rottingdean. The gentlemen, being continually confronted by this feast of female flesh, could only envy when they did not lust, while they pantingly perspired in their black frock-coats, a colour made fashionable for evening wear by George "Beau" Brummell, and wished most heartily that the "Beau" had conceived the idea of making it *de rigueur* to dance in one's shirt-sleeves.

Lucy Briggs-Watson, small, dark and good to look upon, with her peach-bloom cheeks and wide blue eyes, clung to the arm of an extremely apprehensive George, who frequently glanced over his shoulder at Great-Aunt Sophie, almost daring that sharp-tongued female to recognise that he was not her beloved Francis. If George, unhappy in his assumed role of elder brother, half hoped to be unmasked he was out of luck in that quarter. Great-Aunt Sophie was getting more short-sighted by the month, and her great-nephew's features were a blur at any distance greater than six inches.

The old lady, who was William Darker's only sister, leaned heavily on the arm of her eldest son, Randolph Briggs-Watson, Lucy's father, and wheezed up behind the young people. She poked George in the back with her silver-topped cane and demanded to know if he had tried out the Palomino, which she had been certain he would choose, because he was a greedy young rascal and knew very well that his poor old aunt had paid a monstrous heavy sum of money for the beast to that thieving vagabond of a horse-coper at Lewes.

Now it came to it, and with Lucy gazing up at him so adoringly, as though any word that fell from his lips must be a pearl of wisdom, George suddenly found it astonishingly easy to lie. Adopting Francis's easy-going manner he replied, "Tried him over Ditchley Down, Aunt, and he went like the wind. Took fences like a bird and left me with my hind-quarters suspended in mid-air."

Great-Aunt Sophie cackled appreciatively. "Was going to offer him to George until I heard he was joinin' the infantry." She added vindictively, "Just as well I didn't though, because that young fool never did recognise good horse-flesh when he saw it." Her blue, button-bright eyes glinted with malice in the tight, pinched face. How she loved playing one brother off against the other—or trying to—Francis and George rarely reported her more spiteful remarks to each other.

Uncle Briggs-Watson was staring curiously at George's watch-chain. Of 23-carat gold it boasted five flamboyant seals. "Ain't that George's trinket?" he demanded suspiciously, peering closely at the article in question. George coolly returned the bolting gaze of two bloodshot grey eyes which resembled nothing so much as hard-boiled eggs, and lied with aplomb. "George is of the opinion that gold has a more pleasing effect than silver upon a black silk waistcoat. My watch and chain, according to George, must never be worn upon an occasion because they are made of base metal." *Remember in future that every single article we possess must be exchanged. How I shall mourn the loss of my beautiful watch and chain!*

Uncle Briggs-Watson chuckled ferociously. "That is what comes of sucking up to old Lady Branson. George was always her favourite great-grandson. She could not stand the sight of you, Francis, or of Sarah for that matter. She said it was not natural for three to come out of one belly, so she'd only have truck with one." Uncle Briggs-Watson, convulsed by his own wit, doubled up with laughter and would have continued to roar away had not his mother made good use of her cane again to jab him sharply in the ribs.

Another little secret never before revealed thought George. He had picked up one or two interesting items of information concerning his own standing in the family since he had begun his masquerade about three hours ago. After his arrival at Southwood Place to call for Lucy he had twice been referred to by members of the Briggs-Watson ménage as a "dull stick", and Great-Aunt Sophie had angered and shocked him by a reference to "George's impending army career." With a giggle that had chilled his spine she had remarked. "If luck favours you, my dear Francis, he will stop a bullet in Portugal, and you will never have him as a charge upon the Frinton Park estate. Dependent relatives have been the ruin of many a good property . . . bridal jointures . . . annuities. . . ." She had gone rambling on.

A rather more odd effect had manifested itself as a result of the deception, an effect which George had not foreseen. It was distinctly disconcerting, not to say alarming, to be accosted by people with whom one was on very familiar terms and to know that they imagined you were somebody else. It completely stripped a man of his identity, and George experienced the weird feeling that he was standing outside himself looking in. He wondered whether, if he went on being Francis for long enough, he might, in the end, forget that he had ever been George. Now that was a thought to set one's head spinning.

"Where is George tonight?" Uncle Briggs-Watson wanted to know. "Fellow usually turns up, if it is only to make sheep's eyes at Lucy."

The young lady in question blushed, stifled a giggle and looked down at her satin-slippered feet. "I speak the simple truth, m' dear," said her father. "He is madly in love with you." This flattering statement produced a verbal, though not very violent protest. "Oh, Papa, really, you have put me quite out of countenance."

George's love-sick heart gave a great leap at these skittish signs of unease. Could it be that Lucy returned his adoration? This hope was quickly dispelled by her next remark. With her eyes, blue as cornflowers, fixed intently upon his face she said, "I count myself exceedingly fortunate to be betrothed to you, dear Francis. I could never have experienced the least degree of warmth or attachment for poor George."

George felt as though someone was holding a lump of ice against his spine. To cover his embarrassment he muttered something to Uncle Briggs-Watson about George having an invitation to go elsewhere and suggested, "Shall we join the next cotillion, Lucy? See, they are forming up already." Happily, she concurred, and the next minute they were flying over the waxed floor, kicking up little puffs of chalk-dust with their agile feet. George caught a glimpse of Sarah, looking ravishing in a lilac gown trimmed with frills of white lace, who was joining the set on the arm of Dodgson Oliver. By standing on tip-toe and waving his hand George managed to attract Dodgson's eye and mouthed a greeting. Dodgson replied in kind, an amiable smile lighting up his pale, unassuming features. George thought of Dodgson as a comfortable sort of person. He was unfailingly courteous to the ladies, young and old, and never offended his male companions by a careless word or gesture. In this he was very like his father, Lord Frederick, though the latter was somewhat more ebullient by nature and boasted a thatch of carrot-red hair which could light one home on a dark night.

George, marking his sister's sulky expression, the lowered eyes and slightly protruding bottom lip, felt a twinge of impatience with her. She could have done a great deal worse in the matter of a marriage partner, and Dodgson deserved better than to be saddled for life with such a petulant miss. Captain Millars was nowhere to be seen. Undoubtedly he lurked unnoticed behind some pillar or *jardinière*, blissfully unaware of the Darker veto which hung over his well-groomed head, and eagerly awaiting an opportunity to inscribe his name on Sarah's dance card.

Meanwhile, Lucy, gay as a bird in spring, was chattering away about her wedding-clothes, graphically describing her first-day dress, the one she would don immediately after she had discarded her wedding-gown. ". . . and over it I shall wear a blue silk spencer with lace frills at the neck and wrists, and little silver buttons down the front, and my bonnet is to be of pale blue straw, silk-edged and ornamented with white and blue flowers. How do you think I shall look?"

The smiling upturned face set George's stomach churning

and turned his knees to water. Oh, my dearest Lucy, were it not for all these people surrounding us I would take you here and now, and you would not be coy with me any more, my girl, when I had finished with you. He managed to say with solemn sincerity, "I think you will look very well indeed, ma'am, so beautiful in fact that I shall be devilish jealous of any gentleman who dares to accord you so much as a single glance. I do not doubt that I shall be obliged to call out at least six of the swinish fellows before we have been married a week."

This pretty speech took Lucy completely by surprise. She had expected Francis to make some teasing remark about "Fishing for compliments," or "I shall not oblige your vanity, miss," but here he was looking at her so . . . well, so *earnestly*, and speaking in that grave and very *feeling* tone. Was he falling in love with her at last? She had greatly feared that it would never be so. After twelve months of expending all her time and energy towards this single, most desirable objective—that is to say, to make Francis Darker her willing slave—Lucy had almost given up. She decided that further tests of Francis's affection must be made on the instant.

As they clasped hands and side-stepped between the long columns of dancers she smiled brilliantly at George and said, "I should very much like to visit France during our wedding-tour. . . . Oh!"—here Lucy pretended to hesitate, placing a finger to her lip—"did I mention that on a previous occasion?" Of course she had, and she remembered well Francis's reply which had gone something like this: "I should not care to risk this unworthy hide, sweetheart. We might have the misfortune to fall into the hands of Boney, and the French tavern-keepers have the worst reputation in the world for robbing the unsuspecting English traveller. Ask Papa. He will tell you tales that will make you disinclined for foreign travel."

"You may have mentioned it," George was saying carefully. "Did I take to the idea?"

She pouted at him. "Villain, you know that you did not. Now pray do not tease me, Francis. You tried to put me off with stories about being robbed in our beds and having our throats cut, and . . ."

". . . waking up dead?" George interrupted her, laughing heartily. They were at the end of the set now and must part to proceed up the outside of the figure until they reached the top. She could see him smiling at her between the hopping figures of the dancers. Breathless, she faced him again at the top of the set. "Well, sir? Are you going to refuse me again?"

He took her hands in his. "How could I possibly refuse such a delectable little creature anything? We shall go to France, if that is your wish, taking particular care to avoid any contact with Bonaparte and his marauding armies, and you shall go to Paris, and I shall buy you the most splendid hat. It will be the envy of all the ladies here at home. Did I tell you, ma'am, that my hand is itching to untie that lilac bow which fastens your bodice, that my other hand longs to caress the white perfection of your breasts?"

Lucy went bright red and tried to hide her face in her hands, but George's grip was tight and she could not free herself. Her heart was beating very fast and she wanted to open her mouth and suck in large gulps of air. It was not so much that she was shocked by George's wholly unexpected remark. She was too worldly-wise for that. She had seen male and female servants coupling in her father's barn; she had seen elegantly attired gentlemen, red-cheeked from the imbibing of too much claret, tumbling the maids on the back-stairs; through a crack in the door of her father's dressing-room she had seen powdered and perfumed ladies, skirts tucked up to their thighs, sprawled on the bed and babbling incoherencies to faceless gentlemen who heaved up and down like rampant hedgehogs; she had seen two gentlemen doing things behind a curtain which she had never imagined were possible; and she had watched with perfect detachment while one of the servants had killed a noisy pig in the kitchen courtyard. She should have been unshockable. She *was* unshockable. It was just that Francis had never before revealed such blatant signs of lust. He had never so much as kissed her cheek.

Lucy pulled herself together with an effort, patted her shiny brown curls, and with a long sigh of relief came to the conclusion that the victory was hers. She still found this hard to believe when she recalled the hours put in arranging her hair to the best possible advantage, skilfully rouging her cheeks and lips, perfuming her gloves and torturing her waist into a tight little corset which had suddenly exploded upon the fashion scene and was now all the rage, only to be informed by Francis that she looked "pretty fair."

The musicians thumped out the final chords of the cotillion and George, tucking Lucy's arm into his, led her to the side of the ballroom where the buffet tables groaned beneath the weight of the cold collation. He had further surprises in store for her. "Would you have found it impossible to marry my brother George?"

She looked away, and a small, puzzled frown creased her forehead while she fussed with the frills on her white satin gown. Perhaps she had offended Francis by her previous reference to his brother, whom she knew he loved, and the rather patronizing way she had dismissed George as not worthy of her attention. She said doubtfully, "If our parents had insisted. . . ."

"But it would have been a duty rather than a pleasure?"

"Yes."

He offered her a plate and a napkin, and provided himself with similar accompaniments to eating. Together they selected various items from the tables until their plates would hold no more. George thought it amazing that a small girl like Lucy could contemplate eating so much. "How do I differ from Fr. . . . How do George and I differ?" he amended hastily.

The slip passed unnoticed. Lucy's small, puppy-white teeth sank into a pork pasty. Reflective mastication at length produced an answer. "In appearance hardly at all, except that George goes about with a sober countenance while yours is always ready to break into a smile. Indeed, your eyes seem to be smiling all the time."

"And in other respects?" he wanted to know.

She gave a little laugh. "In other respects, sir, you might not be brothers at all. George is an indifferent conversationalist, whereas you are never at a loss for something to say; George is a poor horseman, while you are quite brilliant; George cossets himself when he is ill, but you will never admit to the slightest indisposition."

He said with a wry smile, "George sounds a remarkably dull sort of fellow."

She responded to this with a light shrug. "I hope that I have not offended you. I know that you are very much attached to George."

He smiled broadly. "Yes, I am . . . very attached indeed. He will always have a place in my heart."

"He will make a kind and amiable uncle for our children," Lucy said kindly, trying to make amends.

For a moment George said nothing, plying his fork between mouth and plate and chewing his food with great absorption. Just when she thought that the awkward moment had safely passed he pounced with, "If it had been your fate to marry George, how would you have endured the intimacies of the marriage-bed?" A deliberate attempt to disconcert her followed. "What I mean is, my dear Lucy, if a lady holds a gentleman in as much contempt as you appear to hold my brother George, how is it possible for her to allow him to join his body with hers?"

Looking extremely uncomfortable Lucy replied stiffly, "I am not supposed to know about such things."

"But you do. Come now, Lucy, you do," and as she remained silent and downcast, "You have seen what every child sees in a large household, where men get drunk at parties and women forget their marriage vows."

Tears were not very far away now, and the food on Lucy's plate did not seem to interest her. "Why do you ask such monstrous embarrassing questions? Surely you are not jealous of George?" This last was said with a nervous little giggle which grated on his nerves.

"Not jealous, no, certainly not jealous. Simply curious. George and I were born on the same day, from the same womb, with but five and twenty minutes between our coming into the world. For all I know the midwife may have got us mixed up. George might be the eldest, in which case Francis would be George and George would be Francis."

It was a direct and nicely calculated invitation to unmask him, but no light of understanding or indignation dawned in Lucy's eyes. She was staring at him a little defiantly now, and her voice became querulous as she replied, "I do not like to play games with words, sir. You are talking a parcel of foolish nonsense."

"You have not answered my question."

"I have no recollection of it."

"It cannot have escaped your memory so soon. I shall repeat it. How would you have endured the intimacies of the marriage-bed with poor, *dull* George?"

"I should have shut my eyes and made pretence he was *you!*" She began to eat again, with her eyes resolutely averted. He moved closer to her, forcing her to look up. "Now that is not *nice*, Miss Lucy. It says in the Bible that it is a sin to commit adultery in one's heart."

She looked him straight in the eye and he liked her even better now that she was showing some spirit. "If I did not know you I should declare you to be quite drunk."

"I am drunk . . . with love."

Her eyes flickered uncertainly, then melted into a warm smile of forgiveness. "You *are* jealous! How can you deny it?"

"I do not deny it. I am . . . most damnably jealous."

The relief of that knowledge unloosed her tongue. "Oh, pray do not be, dear Francis. I know it is quite shameless of me to say so, but I do love you very dearly, and to speak truth I find George too glum to suit my taste."

"Poor George," George said bleakly.

"Poor George," she echoed sadly.

Mr William Forth, the Master of Ceremonies, who, all the ladies agreed, could not compare with the late and very much lamented Captain Wade for sheer physical presence, commanded silence with a flourish of his silver baton and announced that His Imperial Majesty Tsar Alexander of Russia having recently set his seal of approval upon the waltz, and having danced it with his Empress at the famous Winter Palace in St. Petersburg, classes would be held at ten o'clock every Tuesday morning, here in the Castle Inn ballroom, for any lady or gentleman who cared to learn the steps at a cost of one shilling and sixpence for one hour's tuition. The names of those interested should be inscribed in the book provided for the purpose in the foyer.

A little buzz of excited speculation followed this announcement, in the middle of which Great-Aunt Sophie tottered up, avid for food and bursting with intelligence. Her yellow, claw-like hand shot out to grasp George by the chin and pull his face down towards hers. "Here is a to-do, Francis. You must go at once to the conservatory. I have just this moment spied that baggage Sarah in the company of a young soldier-boy. They are standing very close to the giant orchids, and he has his arm about her waist." Aunt Sophie paused to catch her breath before wheezing on, "I passed within a foot of them, but they were too much taken up with each other to notice me. If young Dodgson Oliver sees them he will call out the soldier-boy and no doubt get killed for his pains, and that flibberty-gibbet sister of yours is not worth the death of a fine young man. If she were mine I should take her home, whip the skin off her back and feed her on bread and water for a month. I shall tell your Papa so."

George was cursing under his breath. Aunt Sophie was right in one respect. If Sarah was discovered, all hell would break loose, and Dodgson would be looking for another wife. Amiable he might be, but he was too proud to forgive his betrothed for flirting openly with another man. And was it only flirting, or had the thing gone further? Had Sarah been dotty enough to conduct a secret affair right under the noses of her family?

Spurred on by the need for haste, George left Lucy with her grandmother and started to walk casually towards the great glass doors at the south end of the ballroom. These led into a large, marble-floored foyer, which in turn opened out into a conservatory or hot-house, where blooms were nurtured for the great occasions when the Prince Regent held a ball, or a reception for foreign ambassadors in the Pavilion. Visitors to the Castle Inn Assembly Rooms were permitted to inspect the plants, which were protected from the common touch by a wire mesh screen. The jealous custodian of these costly exhibits was Mr Arthur Beaumont, the Regent's Head Gardener.

Before George had time to reach this treasure-house of flora, however, he was waylaid by his mother, who, escorted by none other than Mr Dodgson Oliver himself, had just been to pat the Regent's horses, fifty-four of which splendidly groomed animals were accommodated in the huge circular stables in the grounds of the Pavilion. Assembly Nights at Brighton were full of such curious diversions. "We are looking for Sarah," Claudine said with a nervous little smile. "She was with us in the stables, and now she seems to have disappeared into thin air."

"She said something about being thirsty," Dodgson remarked good-humouredly. "I am sure, ma'am, that we shall come upon her in the ballroom drinking lemonade."

"Er, no. . . ." George's brain was working at a furious

rate as he sought for the words which would protect his sister's reputation. "I have just this minute been informed by Great-Aunt Sophie that Sarah is in the Ladies' Retiring Room, holding a smelling-bottle to her nose. She has a bad headache."

Claudine was staring at her son's watch-chain. A slight frown knitted her brows. "Francis?" she inquired uncertainly. George smiled at her. "I see you are looking at my very splendid watch-chain, Mama. I borrowed it from George."

"Oh, yes, I see." A smile demonstrated Claudine's relief. "I thought for a moment that you were. . . ." Conscious of Dodgson's attentive ears she said cryptically, "You know, that old trick you used to play on me when you were children . . . I thought. . . ."

"We are too old for that sort of thing now, Mama," George assured her with a laugh, and in a moment of inspiration, "Ah, there goes Sarah now, into the garden. She has decided to take the air to clear her head."

Dodgson spun round to face the door. "But she must not venture into the garden alone when it is dark. Where? Where? I do not see her."

"There," George said, pointing confidently at nothing.

"I shall go after her," Dodgson said. "The lanterns do not provide sufficient light to prevent molestation. If you will excuse me, ma'am?"

Claudine nodded rather worried consent, but George quickly laid a restraining hand on Dodgson's arm. "Wait . . . please wait, sir, while I see if Sarah is quite recovered. She would never forgive me if I permitted you to approach her while her hair is in disarray. There is nothing like a headache for spoiling a lady's coiffure." This remark was made with a hard, challenging look at Mama, whose soft dark hair was always perfectly arranged, whether she professed to have a headache or not.

Without bothering to wait for Dodgson to argue further George was off. He stepped outside and was greatly relieved when a quick glance over his shoulder convinced him that his mother and her companion were moving in the direction of the ballroom. Waiting until they had passed through the glass doors he doubled back and headed for the conservatory.

By the time he reached his destination he was sweating profusely, a condition rapidly made worse by the over-powering heat in the huge domed structure which protected "Prinny's" potted plants. One or two people were admiring the plants, passing along the rows of slatted shelves and murmuring their incredulity at some particularly fine bloom. Purple, pink and white orchids paraded before the envious eyes of the ladies and reminded some of the gentlemen of their public school days, and of the sardonic Classics tutor, armed with his whippy little cane—"The Greek word for testicle, young sirs, is *orchis*. Remember that when you are purchasing flowers for the lady who has captured your fickle hearts. Only if she is a *whore* may you present her with an orchid."

George mopped his brow with his pocket handkerchief and peered about him through the masses of foliage. Nothing yet. The conservatory was two hundred feet long. The lovers might be right at the other end of it. He could feel the heat of the under-floor furnace creeping up through the soles of his shoes. If he did not get out of here soon he would imitate the ladies and throw a fit of the vapours.

He was almost at the furthest limit of this massive forcing-house of nature, and was about to turn back with a murmur of frustration, when his eye was attracted by a white-painted door let into the end wall of the building, beyond which could be discerned a small glass structure probably used for the propagation of seedlings. It was worth a moment's investigation. Gingerly he approached and as gingerly placed his hand on the latch, pressing it down and easing the door open with his knee. Exercising extreme caution he inserted his head into the aperture. All his frantic assurances to himself that he would find the place devoid of human occupancy were instantly negated. Sarah and Captain Millars were very much in evidence, their love-making quite adequately illuminated by the light of two candles. George was left in no doubt about the loss of his sister's reputation. Sarah's tumbled skirts and small animal noises outraged his masculine sense of decency. It was not seemly for a lady of quality to behave so. A man might take a whore in that hole-in-the-corner fashion, but a lady might not behave so with her lover; a lady should take care to prostitute herself between silken sheets.

George backed away from the door and jumped as a voice behind him said, "Well, I think she has gone a thought too far this time, do not you?" Dodgson Oliver was looking at George with a queer half-smile on his stricken face, and pushing past him, entered the potting shed, for such it was, while with sinking heart George waited for the inevitable sequel to Sarah's ill-advised "adventure" to take place. He heard his sister give a frightened scream, recognised a challenging male voice, the sound of scrambling bodies and Dodgson saying quite clearly, "You will not refuse to give me satisfaction, sir?" Then came Sarah's sharp, "No, you will be *killed*!" and Dodgson with irony, "Such an event would most certainly settle all your problems for you, would it not, my dear Sarah?"

Miss Pinkerton loses her temper

Miss Emily Pinkerton snuggled up to Francis Darker in the hard wooden bed and complimented him on his "performance." "You was good tonight, Georgie, better'n usual if you doan mind my sayin' so. You was masterful like . . . 'urt me a bit, you know?"

Francis suppressed a smile—one up on George—and leaning across bit her ear. "You was good yourself," he mocked.

Her sharp green eyes slid sideways to look at him. "Doan do that. You know I doan like it. I'm *tryin'* to learn 'ow to talk different now I'm next door to royalty like, and it doan 'elp . . . h . . . elp . . . if you lark about like that."

"Pray accept my apologies. I promise not to do it again." His hand gently massaged her breast and she gave a little wriggle of pleasure, purring like a cat. "Mmmm . . . thass nice. Keep on doin' it."

He was happy to oblige, reflecting as he did so that brother George was a bit of a dark horse. He had been keeping this little morsel up his sleeve for months now, with only occasional references to "my charming milliner friend in Brighton," and never a word about Miss Pinkerton's undeniable attractions.

With a swift movement of her hand Emily pulled aside a cloak of coarse red hair from under her neck. It spread out on the pillow like a gaudy fan, reminding Francis of Raphael's "Drowning Woman."

"I made a 'at . . . h . . . at for Lady H . . . ertford this week," she announced proudly. "She paid seven guineas for it."

"She paid Madame Renée seven guineas for it," Francis corrected her. "How much of that will you get?"

Emily made a chirping sound of impatience. "I'm always tellin' you, Georgie. It's a shilling a 'at and tuppence extra if I 'ave . . . oh, Gawd! . . . *have* to trim it with bird o' paradise feathers. They take a 'elluva long time to fix."

"Seven guineas for Madame Renée, less a shilling or one shilling and tuppence for you. It seems a bit disproportionate, does it not?"

"A bit what?" She screwed up her features into a ferocious scowl. "I wish you wouldn' use them long words."

"A bit unequal," he elucidated. "A bit *unfair*."

"Well a'course it's *unfair*!" she exploded. "You never lissen, do yer, Georgie? I'm always goin' on about it. I thought you was simperthetic like. You *said* you was. You *said* as how you'd get one o' them posh friends o' yours to bring up the matter o' milliners' wages in Parleyment. You *said* it was a cryin' shame that we was paid so low, and now 'ere you are sayin' 'It seems a bit unfair'!" She attempted a passable imitation of his voice and Francis shook with laughter. "Doan do that," he admonished, "yer know I'm tryin' to learn to talk proper!"

Like an angry cat she was at him, and he gave a surprised yelp as she bit his nose. "Fan me, you little bitch!" He leaned over and slapped her face hard, and she flopped back, laughing. "Serves yer right for not lissenin'." Francis, slightly bemused by all this activity, lay back and accused himself of indolence, of not preparing the ground more carefully before venturing upon alien territory with intent to deceive. It was obvious that his brother had developed a rather special relationship with this uncommon little waif from Seven Dials, who had chosen to take up residence in one of the most famous pleasure resorts in England.

He had learned something of her background from George. Her widowed father had moved with his daughter to Brighton in a vain attempt to repair lungs ravished by tuberculosis. Lacking any treatment, save fresh air, for his dread disease, Mr Pinkerton had bowed out of this world six months after arriving in the Prince Regent's playground, and Emily had been left to fend for herself in a cold, hard world which did not recognise a young girl's need for care and protection.

Emily Pinkerton had been just fifteen when she tricked her way into employment at Madame Renée's exclusive establishment in East Street. She had achieved this near-miracle by producing a fake reference written by herself. It purported to come from a high-class milliner in London's Oxford Street who boasted the Royal Warrant. The reference had taken Emily five hours to compose, eight lines of perfect copperplate, each letter of the alphabet painstakingly copied from the letters of a prescription for a sleeping draught supplied by a Brighton apothecary for her father. Including Mr Pinkerton's name and address there had been three lines of writing on the prescription, the whole containing almost every letter of the alphabet. It had been enough. Emily had a big advantage over most girls of her age and condition. She could read and she could draw, and her letter, had Madame Renée but known it, was a carefully executed artistic masterpiece.

The actual content of the letter had been copied, word for word, from the "Ladies' Home Magazine," which frequently gave advice on etiquette and ran a regular feature on the "Composition of Business and Social Correspondence." Emily had had to wait nine weeks before the sort of letter she required was printed in the magazine, and nine consecutive copies of the "Ladies' Home Magazine" had cost her one shilling and sixpence. By the time she had obtained her position with Madame Renée her total wealth had amounted to threepence, and the rent for her small basement room had been due. The landlady, an honest, kind-hearted woman, feeling sorry for the skinny little creature in the black stuff dress, had agreed to wait another week for her money.

Emily had met George Darker when he had accompanied his mother on one of her shopping sprees. While Claudine occupied Madame Renée's time and attention George had spied a diminutive red-haired girl carefully arranging a display of hats in the shop window, placing each exquisite, edible-looking creation on a polished wooden stand. The girl had turned, caught his eye and smiled up at him with an impish lift of her eyebrows which had delighted and at the same time intrigued. George had been enchanted, and having seen Claudine to her carriage, he had forthwith expressed his intention of visiting the Athenaeum Club and waved her good-bye.

After arranging to hire a mount for the return journey, he had hung about Brighton for the rest of that day and having nothing better to do after visiting his Club, had availed himself of the opportunity of patronizing the famous Awsiter Baths which were situated on the western side of Pool Valley, near the beach. The baths were housed in a small, single-storey classical building with pediment, dentil-cornice and round-headed windows, and its façade bore the designation "Hygea Devota". Directly underneath this legend, and infinitely more practical from the point of view of the lowly observer, were inscribed the words "Hot and Cold Baths". Sea-water was pumped into the establishment by means of an engine.

George passed through the portals of this elegant little structure and made discovery of a new and wholly invigorating experience. He was met by toga-ed acolytes who relieved him of his clothes in very short order and marshalled him into a small, steam-filled cavern. There he was deposited unceremoniously upon a tiled bench alongside what looked remarkably like a grossly over-sized lobster. Upon ascertaining that this pink, broiling creature was human, George engaged him in conversation while he waited for his own flesh to assume a similar hue. It transpired that the gentleman in question was a man of the cloth, who declared it as his opinion that poisonous substances must be cast out from his body before his mind could become exercised with the preparation of his Sunday sermon. The idea was a novel one, but in the expounding of it the clergyman proved himself to be a verbose bore and George quickly lost interest in the ethics of inner and outer cleanliness.

After spending about an hour in the great heat of the vapour bath he was placed inside a kind of flannel tent, with sleeves protruding inwards for the convenience of the operator, who placed his arms in the sleeves and proceeded to massage this latest devotee upon every part of his body. This somewhat erotic treatment was followed by a highly-scented hot bath and completed by a cold shower. George was not very much taken up with the latter, but he could not deny that he felt extremely energetic as he paid his money and promised the blonde-haired lady in the glass reception booth that he would most certainly come again.

At eight o'clock that same evening George had returned to the hat shop in order to watch the milliners' assistants pouring out in a chattering stream. He had followed the red-haired girl home, accosting her at the top of her basement stairs and, in the fashion of the day, striking a bargain with her there and then. Emily Pinkerton had agreed to "make herself available" for ten shillings a week, this princely sum entitling George to put in an appearance on any day and at any hour he chose. Appraising her customer with an alert and knowing eye, Emily had assured herself that the occasional present would also be forthcoming.

Their liaison had been successful, both sexually and from the point of view of companionship. The two felt comfortable with each other, and George knew that Emily would fill his masculine needs for as long as he wanted her. To do him justice he took an interest in her affairs and endeavoured to make her drab life more pleasant than it would otherwise have been.

Pondering now upon his own scanty knowledge of Emily, Francis decided that he must not become too involved with her troubles. He had neither the time nor the patience to concern himself with social injustices. The switching of roles with his brother having now become a firm intention, he braced himself to inform her of his impending departure for foreign parts. His earnest ambition had always been to join the army, and he would not give up that ambition without a struggle. Damn his inheritance, and damn Frinton Park, with its incessantly open maw which demanded ever larger infusions of capital. He would not take that burden upon his shoulders.

Emily was muttering to herself about "folks what only 'ave 'alf an ear." He broke through her grumblings. "I am going away soon . . . to join the army. Papa is to buy me a commission."

A protracted silence greeted this information, and then

his hand was removed from her breast and she turned her back on him. Old and childish habits came to Emily's aid when she was upset. She started to gnaw at her fingernails, giving herself time to think. Then, in a voice muffled by the pillow, she said sulkily, "You said you'd try'n get out of it. You said you wasn' goin' if you could 'elp it." No pathetic attempt now to ape the lady in her speech.

"You said, you said," Francis flashed back irritably. "Why must you keep throwing my words in my face? A fellow can say a deuce of a lot and not really mean it."

Emily swivelled round to face him, her small pinched face contorted in a sudden burst of indignant ire. "Oh, so that's it, is it? All them fancy words o' yours about 'elpin' me all you could doan mean a thing. You bloody 'ypocrite. I thought you was white, I reely did."

"No, no, Emily, please. . . ." Francis tried to calm her down. "And the promises I have made to you I mean to keep. Believe me, I do. I shall ride over to Penworth tomorrow and see Papa's friend, Lord Oliver. His father is the Member of Parliament for South Arun and well-known to our family, and he may be able to introduce what they call a Private Member's Bill into Parliament on the subject of milliners' wages."

She was somewhat appeased. "Well, just see you do, thass all. You been talkin' about it for long enough." In order not to appear too easily placated she demanded, "And wot about the dog? Are yer goin' to keep yer promise about 'im?"

"Of course." What about the dog, George? You did not tell me about any dog.

"When?" demanded that relentless, imperious voice.

"When what?"

"Oh, Gawd, you're doin' it on purpose to tease me, ain't you?" She moaned with frustration and kicked him in the shin. "When can I 'ave 'im?"

"Next week, tomorrow if you like," Francis promised recklessly.

"A big 'un?"

"As big as you like." Good heavens, it was like picking one's way through a nest of rattlesnakes. He really must advise George to ring the changes in the whore-houses, instead of practically settling down in domestic bliss with a wife, and handing out pledges in the manner of any hen-pecked spouse. What would she say to trap him next? She said: "One o' them bull mastiffs then. Big bastard like. 'E should be good enough for the job."

"What job?"

The ensuing silence was positively electrifying. He could actually feel the shock waves coursing all down his body. Her voice rose to a screech. "You gorn soft in the 'ead? I *told* you and *told* you. I wanna dog to keep them bleeders from the flash-'ouse up the road out o' my barnet. They keep tryin' to 'tice me in, just to look round like, *they say*, but they'd 'ave me on me back with some fat ole bugger pinnin' me down if I so much as give 'em a wink, or put me foot over the doorstone. That's why I keep on about gettin' 'igher wages. If girls like me was to be paid a proper livin' wage we wouldn' 'ave to go on the streets every night, or fall into the 'ands of them Madams and pimps at the flash-'ouses. We wouldn' 'ave to earn extra money lyin' flat on our backs."

Francis was genuinely appalled. He had never suspected that badly paid young milliners and sempstresses supplemented their meagre incomes in this particular fashion. "But *you* don't have to look for men, Emily," he said apprehensively, almost as though he expected her to contradict him.

"No, I doan," she replied, "but I would 'ave to if it wasn' for you, Georgie, and if you go away it won' do no good my 'avin' a dog, even if 'e is as big as a bloomin' elephant. I'll 'ave to be nice to the flash-'ouse Madam and 'er pretty boys then, and tell the dog to be a good doggie and not to bite the gentlemen's bums 'cos they is goin' to make sure that missus 'as enough gelt to keep body and soul together and doggie in bleedin' bones."

"I shall give you a lump sum before I go and more when I return on leave," promised Francis at once.

"Ow, no . . . o . . . o!" She was off again. "You said you would send me some regular every month, that is if you did 'ave to go, which you didn' know for sure. I doan want money 'angin' about me room just waitin' for anyone to get 'is dirty 'ands on it."

"If I buy you a mastiff no one will dare to come in," Francis pointed out. "The room will be as safe as a bank vault."

"I'd still rather 'ave the money in instalments," she said, "and besides, I gotta take the dog out for walks, 'aven' I? Poor bleeder can' stay cooped up 'ere all 'is life. Gotta relieve 'isself sometimes."

"How much will you need?" he inquired cautiously, wondering how on earth he was going to arrange for the payments to be made without his father knowing. A draft on the bank at Lewes was out of the question since the Manager there, Mr Augustus Wilkins, would be sure to tell Papa that regular monthly sums were going out of his son's account to pay a whore. Out of Francis Darker's account to pay George Darker's woman? He and George would have to use each other's accounts if they decided to proceed with the deception, another small detail neither brother had yet thought of.

"Four sheets a month should do it," Emily was saying.

He was outraged. "A pound a week? Not a penny more than fifteen shillings."

"Done," said Emily, who never looked a gift horse in the mouth, "but if it turns out after you gorn that there's a little stranger on the way I'll 'ave to 'ave more, 'cos I can' live on fresh air."

"You are not with child are you?" he asked worriedly.

"Not as far as I know," she said to tease him, "but then I been careful like, 'aven' I?"

"Have you?" he asked lamely, and wondered what magic she had performed on herself to avoid the processes of procreation. About that she did not intend to enlighten him, but she did not gossip with the flash-house girls for nothing. There were some things, however, that a lady did not discuss openly. "You'll 'ave to go soon," she told him. "I got to git up at five, and I must 'ave a bit o' shut-eye, or me eyes'll feel like toadstools on stalks. There's time for one more if you feel like it." She giggled. "No extra charge to you, Georgie."

This offer was accepted with alacrity and Emily marvelled afresh at the inventiveness Georgie was showing tonight. "'Ere!" she exclaimed, struck by a sudden thought, "you been with one o' them 'igh-class 'ores from the Steine? You never done nothin' like that before. You promised you wouldn', not while you was goin' with me, 'cos the last thing I need is a dose. Oh, Gawd 'elp us, you 'aven', 'ave you, Georgie? You said you wouldn' . . . *you said*. . . ."

Francis was just in time to scramble into the Darker family coach, which was drawing up before the main entrance to the Castle Inn as he came running into Castle Square. Laughing at his near-miss he fell back into the corner seat and surveyed his family, waiting for the usual female clack to begin. Who did what; who wore what; what indelicate, scandalous or amusing things had been said. When all that was forthcoming was a glum, uneasy silence, he guessed at once that something was dreadfully wrong. He put his thought into words. "Is something wrong?"

It was Papa who answered, a strangely angry-looking Papa, who clenched and unclenched his fists, and dug his teeth into his lower lip while he said in measured tones, "Your sister, disobeying the explicit instructions of your mother, which, you may remember, were delivered at the breakfast table this very morning, has disgraced herself. She has been discovered in a compromising situation with

Captain Millars, and there is to be a duel. Naturally Dodgson has retracted his proposal of marriage."

Francis could find no words with which to comment on this shocking intelligence. He accorded his sister a single horrified glance, which she returned with sullen defiance, and for the rest of the journey home scrutinized his boots with the utmost concentration. The old saw, "Least said, soonest mended," ran through his head.

NOVEMBER, 1812

The Die is Cast

Dodgson Oliver, no match for the brilliant swordsmanship of Captain Millars, fell upon the other's weapon in a clumsy attempt to disarm his opponent and was borne from the field of battle—a clearing among the trees near Hollingbury Camp at Brighton—with, in the words of Mercutio a wound ". . . not so deep as a well, nor so wide as a church door, but 'twill be enough. . . ." Dodgson expired before his seconds could get him to the waiting carriage.

Captain Millars, staring ruefully at the blood-stained blade, walked slowly away with his seconds and was seen no more. Dodgson had sacrificed his life for certain idealistic notions held by many gentlemen of the period, and James Darker could never find it in his heart to forgive his daughter, whom he regarded as being directly responsible for the death of his best friend's only son.

A bare three weeks after Dodgson had been laid to rest in the Oliver family mausoleum at Penworth, the schoolmaster of Piddingfold village, a clerical gentleman with ideas above his station, took advantage of the shame which had fallen upon the Darker household, elaborated details of which had quickly circulated round the county, and presenting his dog-eared card at Frinton Park one gloomy November morning, had the temerity to ask James if he might have leave to call upon Miss Darker as an "interested party".

It was over three years now since Mr Sidney Cobbett had first cast covetous eyes upon the fair Miss Darker, with her pale complexion and her small, rosebud mouth, which seemed to smile exclusively for him when he ventured to engage her, suitably chaperoned, in conversation. At the Piddingfold monthly assemblies, held in the long room above the "Blue Boar" inn, Mr Cobbett had experienced the first pangs of love, and the joy of touching hands with the beloved, which sent little electric thrills, starting from his boots, right up to his neck, where they terminated in a dull red flush.

As the dance progressed Miss Darker would ask all the proper questions concerning the conduct of his school and the academic abilities of his children. He would respond with earnest enthusiasm, and with a wealth of detail which soon had his unenraptured audience of one vainly endeavouring to conceal a yawn. In fine then, Mr Cobbett worshipped Miss Sarah Darker and she, quite oblivious of the havoc she wrought in his narrow breast, treated him in the same polite and distant manner which his status as a lower-class professional, albeit a highly respectable one, merited. Mr Cobbett had long ago resigned himself to the fact that his goddess stood upon the summit of unscaleable heights, and was content merely to adore from afar.

Then, like a bolt from the blue, the goddess revealed her feet of clay. Rumour had it that she had been discovered in a compromising situation—happily Mr Cobbett had no idea just how compromising, for Dodgson was dead and the lips of George and Captain Millars were sealed—with a man other than her betrothed, and her reputation lay in shreds. By a sudden turn of fortune's wheel he, Sidney Cobbett, the humble school-master, would actually be doing Miss Sarah Darker a favour by offering her his hand in marriage.

James Darker conducted Mr Cobbett into the library, heard him out, and after the briefest of pauses, gave his consent to a formal wooing. With a stern and cynical eye bent upon the flushed face of this village pedagogue, James offered a dowry of £3,500—quite sufficient to maintain style in a modest four-roomed cottage—and suppressed a grim smile as Mr Cobbett expressed his heartfelt thanks at such a generous offer.

Surprisingly, Sarah made no objection when her father informed her that he had given Mr Cobbett permission to call on her. Only Claudine suspected the truth, that her daughter was already trapped by the biological processes taking place inside her. A child had been conceived in a potting shed at Brighton, and not only must Sarah receive Mr Cobbett with a welcoming smile, but she must hurry him on a little, in order that he might provide a convenient cloak for her bastard. After it was born she would plan her escape. An eternity of years to be spent at the side of the odious Mr Cobbett, with his bad teeth, his foul breath, and his sly, secretive eyes concealing God knew what lechery, was not to be borne.

Sarah had never thought it possible that she could ever come to hate Papa, but hate bred hate, and he had been the first to sew the seed. His friendship with Lord Frederick, of very long standing, had triumphed over the tragedy which she had unwittingly brought about, but there must be a scapegoat and she had been firmly cast in that role. Mentally Sarah ran through the list of her aunts and decided that Aunt Augusta would be the one most likely to offer an errant niece protection. Domiciled in London, and mixing in the very best society, Augusta would find a niche for a disgraced female relative and maybe even help her to obtain a divorce.

At first Sarah had thought she might go to London straight away, throw herself on the mercy of her aunt, and enlist her help in getting her child farmed out to some worthy family. That way she would never be forced to share a bed with Mr Cobbett and submit to embraces which could never be anything but distasteful and repellent. The more sensible course was to stay, wait until her baby was born, and make her escape when the time was right.

Sensible, because a woman living apart from her husband was slightly more acceptable in society than one who had borne an illegitimate child whose paternity was uncertain. Sarah, after a prolonged struggle with herself, decided to stay. She could not escape the irony of her situation. She had not looked forward to marriage with Dodgson. How much less would she relish the prospect of being locked within that solemn institution with Mr Cobbett.

It seemed to Sarah that the Darker women were doomed to make indifferent marriages. Her Aunt Amelia had married an apothecary; her Aunt Sarah a grocer; Aunt Caroline had lost her heart to a sea-captain; and Aunt Elizabeth had become the wife of a country vicar. Only Augusta, as her name would seem to imply, had climbed to Olympian heights, and married a wealthy baronet who spent most of his time in the London coffee houses and clubs, and the rest fast asleep on a back bench of the House of Commons. She must pin her faith on Augusta and make a resolution to endure for the next twelve months or so. She hoped most fervently that Francis and George were as firm in their intention to escape from the ties that bound them. Life was so dreadfully unfair, and it was up to the individual to redress the balance as far as possible. Her brothers' decision would be revealed that very morning after breakfast, when the conspirators had agreed to meet in the Morning Room, while Papa immersed himself with unrelieved gloom in the monthly accounts and Mama had a conference with her dressmaker.

The trio which assembled in the Morning Room did so in subdued silence. A month ago the young Darkers had been suffering from a simple case of wet-day boredom. Lacking anything exciting to do, they had explored forbidden realms; now they were pre-occupied and vaguely apprehensive as to what the future might hold. Sarah had adopted a rather studied air of resignation, seeing herself as a human sacrifice offered up to appease the gods for the death of Dodgson Oliver, whom she now somewhat belatedly regarded as the sweetest, kindest, most worthy person who had ever lived.

George, for his part, sometimes found it difficult to meet his sister's eye, for superimposed upon her face would always be the image of her languishing in the arms of Captain Millars. It would be a long time before that unpleasant picture faded from his mind. After three weeks of Lucy Briggs-Watson's undivided attention he had greatly gained in enthusiasm for their enterprise, his only fear being that Francis might want to back out.

As for Francis, he knew that he could never marry Lucy Briggs-Watson, not even with a shot-gun pressed firmly into his back. All he wanted to do was to get away for a while to plan his future. It would never be possible to marry Emily Pinkerton, of course, because she was too far beneath him to be acceptable by the family, but he did nurse the hope that she would be waiting for him each time he came home on leave from his regiment, still willing, for the sum of fifteen shillings per week, to cater to his needs.

All three sat down, and it seemed a long time before anyone said anything, though in fact it was less than a minute before Sarah broke the silence, her voice pitched to a cool, challenging note. "Well, you have made up your minds I suppose?"

"I am game," said Francis at once, and from George, "Yes, I think so, provided that Francis is absolutely sure about the question of the inheritance. Once I am married to Lucy there can be no turning back. You do see that?" A look of anxious intensity was directed at his brother.

Francis shrugged. "If I inherit I must take on Lucy and all the responsibilities of the estate. As the heir I shall also be responsible for any members of the family who have no means of subsistence, and are dependent on small annuities and grants. I do not think I can carry that weight upon my shoulders. You, George, are better equipped mentally to undertake the care of the family."

He grinned cheerfully. "I know that you will never let me starve if I return from the wars minus a leg or an arm. In any case, I am of the opinion that every man should make his own way in the world. If a man has an assured future from birth he is never likely to get up off his backside and shift for himself. Everything is there, ready and waiting for him."

"Not quite," George argued. "Papa virtually inherited Frinton Park when Grandpapa became too old to run the estate, but he has to work like a dog to keep it going."

"And that is just what I mean," riposted Francis. "For my part, I should be more than willing to work like a dog at something I had created for myself, but when one inherits, a lot more than money falls into one's lap. Young George Lambton over at Glynwood has to pay three jointures all told, one to his grandfather's widow, who is not his own grandmother, one to his Mama, and a third to an aunt who has a reversionary claim on the estate . . . and now there is talk of landowners having to pay one shilling and sixpence in the pound for something the government call Income Tax."

"I suppose," George said thoughtfully, "that we keep these things going for the sake of our children?"

"Why do we not allow our children to fend for themselves?"

"Because they are a part of us, and they carry our seed from generation to generation."

"Generation to generation," boomed Francis, in fine imitation of Parson Butts, who cared for the Piddlingfold flock. They all laughed, and for the first time the tension in the Morning Room was eased. George said, "It is true, of course, that one is pressured from birth into doing things one would much rather not do, simply because one's parents keep on about duty and respect and family unity. Take Francis, for instance. He agreed to marry Lucy because Great-Aunt Sophie liked him better than she likes me and badgered him into it. After a while it was too late to back out without causing a great deal of fuss.

"If you had said a firm "No" in the first place, Francis, old Sophie would have grumbled and threatened to cut you off from her society, and talked a lot of foolishness about ungrateful brats, and then she would have given up, and you would have been free to marry elsewhere. Our parents are still trying to perpetuate the myth of the marriage of convenience."

"It is not a myth!" argued Sarah angrily. "My marriage to Dodgson was arranged between Papa and Lord Frederick, and now I am made to feel like a murderess."

"You should have refused Dodgson when he proposed," said George sternly, "and you should have had more sense than to conduct an affair with a penniless adventurer like Millars."

Sarah pouted and looking down at her clasped hands said, "I was not conducting an affair. I danced with him a few times, that is all, and his conversation made me laugh. I had no idea that he was going to . . . take advantage of me like that."

"He proposed to you, did he not?" George challenged relentlessly. "You should have resisted his advances, and you did not have to walk into that confounded potting shed with him. From my observation it did not appear that you were putting up any great show of resistance."

A charged atmosphere was building up again. Francis intervened quickly, "Do you remember Papa speaking of Aunt Amelia? Grandpapa arranged for her to marry an old man who died on the very day of their wedding."

"So she followed the dictates of her own heart, or so they say, married the village apothecary, and has been miserable ever since," Sarah said. "I must own that hers is a case where freedom of choice did not lead to happiness, but it is always the exception which proves the rule."

George said with conviction, "Of one thing I am quite certain. Marriage, whichever way you look at it, is a gamble."

"The whole of life is a gamble," philosophized Francis.

"So you are going ahead with the plan?" put in Sarah, bringing her brothers back on course. "At least you will be shaping your own destinies."

Nothing more was said. The three continued to sit, feeling somehow rather foolish and a little depressed. Francis and George could find no more arguments with which to bolster up their reckless decision. Sarah could find no possible excuse for the way she had behaved. They were each about to launch a craft upon uncharted seas, in the midst of which more than one hidden reef would be encountered.

JUNE/JULY, 1814

Miss Pinkerton goes into business

George Darker had achieved the summit of his ambition, or thought he had, when he married Lucy Briggs-Watson in the parish church of Piddingfold village. The bridal bouquet, according to Darker family custom, had been placed on the grave of Cousin Patience Westlake, "departed this life on the ninth day of June, in the year of Our Lord, 1770" . . . at the end of a hangman's rope. The mystery surrounding Patience, which had now taken on the colour and embellishment of legend, had remained a mystery for years. Originating when William Darker was a young man, and but newly married to Clarissa Branson of Varracombe Hall, the affair of Patience Westlake had created a scandal in the county which was long remembered. William's children had been protected by a conspiracy of silence from learning the truth, but the tale, with various additions and exaggerations, was out now, and the triplets had come to regard Patience as something of a folk heroine, for she had murdered their uncle who was a "black sheep".

Lucy's brave Lenten lilies and early, pale pink wake-robins had made a bright splash of colour on the small mound close to the churchyard wall, mingling with the buttercups and daisies which sprang up year after year like a protective coverlet to hide a young woman's bones. Lucy had been a beautiful, radiant bride in her white satin gown decorated with blue true lovers' knots, and George had considered himself the luckiest fellow alive, visualizing a golden future surrounded by the laughing faces of his children, faces which would, of course, be completely eclipsed by the tender and loving looks of that most perfect of beings who was now his wife.

The rosy vision had faded almost overnight, for no sooner had Lucy exchanged her wedding-gown for her first-day gown of pale cream taffeta, trimmed with coffee-coloured ruched ribbon, than she had begun to display the more calculating side of her nature, a side which neither George, nor Francis for that matter, had ever suspected existed. Lucy Darker, after returning from her wedding tour, which had included the promised trip to Paris, had directed all her energies towards ousting Claudine from her position as the mistress of Frinton Park in order that she, Lucy, might assume that important role herself.

Claudine, by no means ready to abdicate, firmly resisted all attempts to wrest from her the household keys, and a clash of personalities had ensued for which Lucy roundly blamed George. As his father's heir he should have been able to relegate his mother to her proper status in life which, according to Lucy, was that of dowager. The term dowager as applied to Claudine was singularly inappropriate. In her elegant clothes and wickedly provocative hats, the latter covering a head in which no single grey hair could yet be discerned, she could have passed for Lucy's sister. Lucy knew it and was not pleased. She began to nag her husband, and in no time at all George's ravishing little creature, with her pretty, coquettish airs, had turned into a hard-faced, sharp-tongued virago. A strange reversal of nature had taken place. The bright, gay butterfly had gone back into its chrysalis, its colourful gossamer wings transmuted into drab grey.

To add to George's increasing wretchedness Lucy showed no signs of becoming fruitful, and a year after their marriage he was still without his longed-for first-born. Claudine made the usual trite remarks about there being "plenty of time", and "adjusting to the married state", but George had the uneasy feeling that in this too he was to be cheated. It was not long, therefore, before he had begun to envy Francis, who had already fought in one victorious engagement at Castella, and had now been promoted to the rank of Captain. Francis's letters home spoke of the exhilaration of going into battle, and of the aftermath, when beautiful Portuguese and Spanish ladies devoted themselves to the pleasant exercise of making the lives of the English officers happy. On one memorable occasion he had actually dined in the company of the Earl of Wellington, who had kindly lent him his hunting dogs for an afternoon's sport.

To think, George had sighed to himself, as he perused his brother's letters, that my present unhappiness all came about because I was bored on a Friday afternoon back in October, 1812. A burning desire to resume his own identity began to harass him, but he knew that for the time being nothing could be done in that direction. Would it ever now be possible once again to change places with Francis? His mistake, he realised, had been in marrying Lucy before he had really come to accept and relish the idea of becoming Francis. He did not *feel* like Francis. He felt like George and thought that it would ever be so.

One morning in June of the year 1814, just over a year after his marriage, George was preparing to ride into Lewes to buy a new saddle when a footman informed him that a young person was at the front door requesting to see him. The person in question was a young female of the servant class and had no card. She had given her name as Miss Emily Pinkerton.

This intelligence filled George with a nameless dread. He had firmly closed the door upon that chapter of his life when he married Lucy. Sometimes, often indeed of late, he had begun to wish that it were not so, but since everyone supposed, including Emily, that George Darker was fighting for King and country in the foothills of the Pyrenees, it would not have been possible for him to resume his acquaintanceship with the fascinating milliner. What on earth can she want, George asked himself? Supposing me to be Francis, what possible business can she have with me?

Miss Emily Pinkerton, pacing the front hall, and looking very trim and neat in her blue pelisse and yellow straw bonnet, was in a similar state of uncertainty, for she was still debating within herself exactly how much money she could expect to extract from George Darker in return for her sworn promise never to reveal to a living soul, more particularly to his wife, that there was an imposter at large. It occurred to Emily, now that she was actually within the walls of Frinton Park, that she was taking a very great risk in coming at all, because it was very much on the cards that she might have the ill-luck to encounter other members of the Darker family, notably Mrs Lucy, who would demand to know her business, and probably turn her out of doors without her ever having seen the person she had come to visit.

It was a risk she had been forced to take. A note, sent through the post, might well have been torn up and disregarded, or even placed in the hands of the county justices if there had been so much as a hint of blackmail in it. Emily never liked to put anything in writing. You just never knew when a thing like that might pop up and bite you. If accosted by young Mrs Darker, or perhaps by the elder Mrs Darker, she could always say that she was setting up in business as a milliner on her own account, and was out looking for customers. If she added that she had made hats for Lady Hertford it would make a great impression and testify to her extreme respectability. Was not Lady Hertford the Prince Regent's mistress, and what could be more genteel than that?

It was, in fact, quite true that Emily intended to go into business on her own account, but not quite in the way one might suppose. She had a very different purpose in mind for any money she might be able to squeeze out of George Darker. It was funny really. She had liked him once, quite a lot. There was a time when she would never have dreamed of treating him so shameful. Then he had practised that very nasty little deceit on her, all because he wanted to marry his brother's fiancée, and for that she would never forgive him. For that he would pay.

The footman returned, and with what Emily described to herself as a "smell-under-the-nose" look, instructed her to follow him. Meekly she obeyed, looking about her curiously at this "gentry" mansion, which she had never seen before except in her imagination. The interior beauties of Frinton Park were, alas, lost to Emily Pinkerton's unawakened eye; the intricate plaster mouldings on the ceilings, picked out in gold leaf; the Italian marble fireplaces; the paintings; the porcelain, and the furniture; and above all, the marvellous collection of Venetian glass which James Darker had brought back from his Grand Tour of Europe. Gaudiness was the only thing that pleased Emily's outward eye; her inner eye already saw the gold paint and red plush which would adorn the rooms of her new business premises.

George was waiting to receive her in the Morning Room, shrewdly judging that the formality of the Saloon would be utterly lost on Emily and would have no "quelling" effect whatsoever. He stood stiffly upright in the exact centre of the Aubusson carpet, hands clasped behind his back. His frock-coat, which he would instantly have donned to receive a lady, was draped carelessly across the arm of a chair. The buff pantaloons—a style made fashionable by the Prince Regent—and the orange waistcoat of ribbed silk which he wore both belonged to Francis.

Emily advanced boldly into the Morning Room, extending her small gloved hand. George touched his fingertips to hers in a perfunctory salute. The slight did not seem to disconcert her, if indeed she noticed it. "Mr Francis Darker?" she inquired cheerfully, and upon receiving a cautious nod, "Yes, of course you are. You couldn' be anyone else, could you? You're as like Georgie as a pea in a pod."

Two peas in a pod. That was how Sarah had described her brothers. On the lips of Emily, a new, rather more pert than usual Emily, George found the simile faintly distasteful. Now that he saw her again after all these months he had a chance to take a more objective view of the little milliner. There stood before him a seventeen-year-old girl, under-sized for her age, dressed in sober and genteel fashion, with her red hair kept firmly under control by the use of a considerable quantity of pins. She might have been applying for a position as a parlour-maid . . . until one looked into her eyes, which showed not the slightest indication that she was begging for approval. No prospective parlour-maid had ever entered Frinton Park—by the front door, if you please—with that particular air of gay insouciance. George felt not the least desire to renew his relationship with Emily. The old intimacy was gone for ever. "Will you sit down?" he offered politely, and indicated a comfortable arm-chair.

"Thanks," said she, accepting the offer with alacrity. A black silk reticule hung from Emily's arm. She removed it and placed it beside her feet. Her blue cotton gloves were daintily peeled off and deposited carefully on top of the reticule. She looked up. "I s'ppose you're wonderin' why I'm here?"

He tried a somewhat distant if courteous smile and took a chair facing hers. "Miss Emily Pinkerton, if I heard my man correctly. Were you not acquainted with my brother George?"

"We were very well acquainted," she agreed, smiling back at him and tilting her head a little to one side, like a bird listening for a worm. "You might say we were very much attached to each other."

The sly suggestiveness of her manner angered George. Anxious to be done with this interview, and to send Miss Emily Pinkerton about her business, he asked rather sharply, "Is it money you need, Miss Pinkerton? Did not my brother provide for you before he left for Portugal?"

"Ow yes, sir, he did!" Emily's green eyes widened as if to

say, "How could you possibly think that a gentleman would not make proper provision for his doxy?"

"Well then?" He was frowning now, his brows drawn together in a tight little knot of irritation. She smiled disingenuously. "Well, it's like this, you see. I reckoned like that it shouldn'a been him what was made to pay. It should'a been the man what was enjoyin' my favours permanent like, and that was you, wasn' it, Georgie?"

Her surprise attack was perfectly timed. She saw an instant reaction mirrored in the startled eyes and slackening mouth, which proved to her beyond doubt that she had hit upon the truth. She had been very sure. The unexpected birth-mark had been proof positive in itself and you cannot perform acts of intimacy with a man over a period of months and not *know* him, right down to the very marrow of his bones.

Even as he struggled to profess bewilderment at her question George's confused brain registered the fact that Emily's speech had slightly improved. It was obvious that she had been trying very hard indeed. The bad grammar and broad, whining vowels of the cockney were still there, strong and dominant, but the aspirates had been firmly dealt with.

"My name is Francis," George said, with as much dignity as he could muster, "but only my friends are permitted to address me so familiarly. The rest call me Mr Darker."

"Oh, yes? Well, *Mr Darker*, you're a bleedin' liar you are!"

Ah, so she forgot herself when she was out of temper. That was a sign of weakness which he might be able to turn to his own advantage. He tried again, still with that superior air of a gentleman dealing with a troublesome doxy. "If I am to be insulted in my own house, accused of being other than I am, may I know upon what grounds you base your ridiculous accusation?"

Her eyes, confident and unafraid, twinkled with amusement. "You're different, Georgie. You know that? You was never all up-stagey with me. You never talked down to me like. I thought you liked me. I reely did. I thought you had what they call a soft spot, just for little Emily, until you pulled that bleedin' rotten stroke and sent Francis to try and make out he was you."

Very slowly, almost indolently, in the manner of any fine lady, she untied the strings of her bonnet. ."Thass better. I can' stand nuthink under me . . . my chin. Makes me want to puke. As I was sayin', I knew when you pulled that trick that you didn' care for me, but I couldn' think why you done it. Then I read about Mr Francis Darker marryin' Miss Lucy Briggs-Watson . . . in the "Courier" it was, and it didn' half give me a turn, but it all come clear to me, 'cos I remember your sayin' as how Francis didn' want to get married and wished he could go for a soldier like you. It all come together like then. D'ye see?"

Weakly he surrendered to the inevitable, knowing that she would never have come all this way to see him if she had not been absolutely certain of her facts. "How did you find out?"

Her answering grin was positively triumphant. He was easier game than she had thought he would be. "Lottsa things give . . . gave you away, Georgie. You was never all that excitin' as a lover, until one night when you come . . . came to Brighton and I thought you was Astley's circus all rolled into one. You was all over me, doin' things I didn' think you knew about. It ain't half funny was what I thought to meself at the time, but nuthink clicked like until you started doin' other little things what was wrong. You combed your hair different, pulled on your boots different, and you didn' make the usual little jokes, the ones as is private between us, you know? It was lottsa things, Georgie."

"But you cannot *prove* anything," put in George, beginning to think that he had fallen too easily into the trap she had set for him. Her eyes narrowed. "Oh no, Georgie. I can' prove nuthink . . . not without makin' you blush that is, 'cos only your Ma and Pa and Francis and Mrs Lucy knows about that big 'airy mole you got on your bum, and Mrs Lucy doan know that Francis *hasn'* got a mole on 'is . . . his bum, leastways she doan till I tell her."

It was nightmarish, this crude exchange in the Morning Room. Nothing like it had ever before been heard inside the walls of Frinton Park he was sure. "So, it is blackmail," he said, and his heart sank, for he knew that that was a thing which went on for ever and ever.

She was nothing if not forthright. "Yes, it's blackmail, Georgie, or a little compensation like, for that lousy stunt you pulled."

"How much?"

"Two and a half thousand," she responded promptly.

"He was aghast. "I haven't got that much money."

"Miss Lucy come to you without a dowry then?" she inquired with an impertinent lift of her eyebrows which made him want to slap her. He tried to keep his voice under control as he replied, "No, but Papa has the disposal of Mrs Darker's dowry, not I."

Despite his anger at her avarice he was curious. "What shall you do with such a large sum of money? I thought you had an aversion to lump sums."

"I'm gonna spend this lot straight away."

"On what?"

"A flash-house,"—and before the spark of astonishment in his eyes had died away—"I'm gonna be a Madam, with a fancy flash-house, employing twenty or so girls, and I'm gonna keep me own carriage and pair, and live in a tip-top house in the Steine, as near to Mrs Fitzherbert's place as I can get it."

He exploded with contempt. "You bloody little hypocrite! You were always rattling on to me about the flash-houses in Brighton, and how they exploit little girls of eleven and twelve, purchased from parents who could not afford to feed them."

She countered this attack with an expression bordering on primness. "*My* house'll be different. I'm havin' no one under fifteen workin' for me."

"So I am to finance a whore-house?"

"Thass right," she agreed cheerfully, "on'y I'm callin' it a palace o' pleasure."

He responded with an unmirthful bark of contempt. "Hah! And if I refuse to finance your *palace of pleasure*?"

The prim look was gone, to be immediately replaced by one of grim resolution. "Mrs Lucy finds out you ain't Francis, but baby brother Georgie, and that you played a dirty trick on her too."

George could not bear to sit looking at her any longer, at the pale, acquisitive face which had once so enchanted him, because then it had looked merely pathetic, with the green eyes begging to be loved; and at the thin little mouth which had offered itself for his kiss. He rose to his feet. Hands in the pockets of his pantaloons he moved about the room, feeling depressed that one with whom he had established such a carefree, easy relationship should now be turning on him like a treacherous dog. He was honest enough to admit to himself, however, that it was he who had destroyed that relationship in the first place by trying to deceive her. She had trusted him implicitly and he had let her down. "I cannot even sell a horse," he mused aloud. "They all belong to Papa, except Great-Aunt Sophie's Palomino, and she only gave him to Francis on condition that he did not sell the animal."

"You'll get the money, Georgie," she consoled brightly. "You just gotta put your thinkin' cap on."

"How long have I got to raise it?"

She appeared to consider the matter and at length declared, "A month. Now thass pretty white of me, innit? I could'a said a week. You come and see me a month today at North Street and we'll still be the best o' friends."

Suddenly he wanted her out of the house. Quite roughly he yanked her to her feet, retrieved her reticule, snatched up her gloves and thrust these articles into her hand. Then he pushed her towards the door. With his hand on her elbow he opened the door and ran smack into Lucy.

His wife's face wore its now habitual expression of extreme irritation. "Oh, there you are, Francis. Mama says that I may not have the carriage today because. . . ." She broke off as her eyes took in Emily. "Who is this?" Instant recognition that the "person" was not a lady. Trust Lucy for that. "Persons" were not formally introduced. George therefore said, "Her name is Miss Emily Pinkerton. She has come to see Mama about a hat. One of the servants showed her in here instead of taking her up to Mama."

It was not bad for the spur of the moment. "Oh, I see." Lucy lost interest. "Well, will you please go and speak to Mama about the carriage? I must have it this morning to visit because I particularly want to see Grandmama. I suppose you had better take Miss . . . er, Pinkerton up with you, but do not allow Mama to become totally absorbed in a discussion of hats until you have settled the matter of the carriage. I shall be in the Eating Room." Without a further glance at Emily she was gone.

Emily's face was as innocent as a baby's as she inquired, "Did you change places with Francis just to get that, Georgie?"

George had no one in whom to confide his troubles except Sarah, so, on the afternoon of Emily Pinkerton's visit he rode down to the village and turned his horse into the small green lane which led to the four-roomed cottage attached to the school-house. A wailing drone coming from inside the latter, a long, low building surmounted by a bell-tower, and with a gilded weather-vane twirling merrily round and round in the boisterous south-westerly breeze, told him that the youth of Piddingfold had their noses firmly set to the grindstone. He paused for a moment to listen and could just make out the seven times table squeaked forth in ragged unison.

Leaving his horse to crop the grass in the school-master's front garden, George made his way up the flagged path between borders of white alyssum and blue ageratum, and circling the cottage entered the unpretentious dwelling by the back door. This was always left open unless the entire household, consisting of Mr and Mrs Cobbett, their baby son Thomas, Cook and Lizzie, the parlour-maid, were from home. Confident that his brother-in-law was safely occupied in the school-house, from whence his tottering charges, heads bursting with knowledge, would not emerge for at least another hour, George passed through the back kitchen, exchanging a greeting with Cook, and went from thence into the front parlour.

There he came upon his sister, lounging upon a sofa and deeply engrossed in "Pride and Prejudice," a novel by a lady, which had recently exploded upon the English scene to delight the population. It was not the sort of occupation one might have expected a school-master's wife to be performing at three o'clock of a week-day afternoon, when she should have been receiving the good wives of Pidding-fold village, pouring tea and listening with rapt attention to an account of their offsprings' academic progress. It must be remembered, however, that Mrs Sarah Cobbett was a lady, and just as she had no intention of soiling her hands with common household tasks, neither would she entertain in her parlour those whom she considered to be her social inferiors.

Mr Cobbett frequently upbraided his wife for dereliction of duty, quoting Scripture at her to point out the wickedness of sloth and the sin of pride, but she remained coolly aloof from these proseletyzings, inciting him to anger by the remoteness of her expression and, when she deigned to answer his accusations at all, which was seldom, the distant contempt in her tone.

The lust with which Mr Cobbett had originally ap-proached the marriage-bed had now dwindled to an occasional, rather desperate assertion of his conjugal rights, which left him unsatisfied and his wife even more contemptuous, if that were possible, than before. The school-master had struck a bad bargain, and since he could do nothing to get himself out of it, he made doubly certain that she who was the cause of his present misery should suffer too. He kept Sarah short of money, a meanness which infuriated her because the locked wooden chest in the spare bedroom contained three thousand five hundred pounds in gold, handed over to Mr Cobbett on the day of her wedding by her father. Not one penny of it had her husband spent. Every Saturday night he would repair to the small, sparsely furnished room—apart from the chest it contained only a bed and a chair—and proceed to count his hoard, sometimes adding a coin or two of his own which he had saved out of the seven pounds fifteen shillings which he withdrew from his house-keeping bag on the first day of each month for his family to live on.

To Sarah he gave no money at all, ordering all the food for the small household himself, and if his wife required so much as a button or a ribbon she must ask him for the wherewithal to buy it. Grudgingly he would count out the amount required into her stiffly extended palm and question her closely afterwards as to the exact cost of the article she had purchased. Had it been one shilling or only elevenpence three-farthings? He thought the latter, for he had seen that particular quality and colour of ribbon clearly priced in the window of the haberdasher's. Mr Wellings, the present owner of the old-established Smith's Emporium, was always very careful in such matters, and his price tags, written in perfect copperplate style, could be made out at a distance of ten yards. Where, Mr Cobbett frequently demanded, unwisely ignoring the scream in Sarah's eyes, was his farthing change?

As to the baby, Mr Cobbett eyed this lively infant somewhat askance, suspecting, because of young Thomas's premature arrival, that he could not lay claim to the title of father. The suspicion made him more sour than ever, and there were occasional dark references over supper to Sarah's "unfortunate" past. Sarah bore it all with hard-won fortitude, biding her time, awaiting an opportunity to break into that locked box in order that she might present herself at Aunt Augusta's house in Charlotte Street with a respectable sum to her name. If her husband chose to run after her and accuse her of theft, Aunt Augusta would deal with him in very short order. Once among wealthy, influential relations she would be safe.

Sarah greeted her brother with a smile in which relief was mingled with genuine delight. "George! How very glad I am to see you. It is quite safe," she assured him quickly, noting his look of alarm as she pronounced his name. "Cook is deaf and Lizzie is gone down to the dairy." Laying aside her book she motioned him to a chair and rose to pour him a glass of Madeira—an extravagance which not even Mr Cobbett could prevent since George supplied it free of charge. After the performance of this office she resumed her previous position on the sofa, and having at once descried the look of anxiety on her brother's face, restrained herself from launching into a full-scale indictment of Mr Cobbett and his latest "atrocity".

"Is Lucy being difficult again?"

He shook his head. "No, not Lucy," and then he told her, in flat, unequivocal terms, of the visit of Emily Pinkerton. After an initial expression of horror and surprise Sarah inquired, "What do you mean to do?"

George confessed that he had little idea. That is why he had come to see her. Two heads were better than one. He had, he told her, about twenty-five pounds to his name in the bank at Lewes, and no more would be added to that paltry sum until his next month's allowance of thirty pounds was placed to his credit by Papa.

While her brother was speaking Sarah's mind gradually drifted elsewhere, until it became firmly concentrated upon a certain locked wooden chest which she judged was situated almost directly above her head. Involuntarily she glanced up at the ceiling as George mused aloud upon various avenues which might be explored in pursuit of the enormous sum of two thousand five hundred pounds.

Abruptly Sarah broke through her brother's vague suppositions to ask, "Should you like to commit a robbery?" The smile on her face as she posed the question must surely mean that she was not in earnest, but when she went on to explain about the wooden chest, and her husband's miserly refusal to be parted from a single penny piece of her dowry, George quickly perceived that she had never been more serious in her life.

"It would have to be done when we were all away from home," pursued Sarah. "I could let you know the most convenient time." After a pause, during which George continued to regard her with a rather doltish stare, she exclaimed excitedly, "Next week! We are to visit Mr Cobbett's sister at Little Dole on Tuesday, and Cook and Lizzie shall have the day off."

George pulled his wits together and came to the conclusion that he was not so much shocked by the proposal itself as by the suddenness of it, combined with the knowledge that Cobbett had not deposited Sarah's dowry in the bank. With this last thought uppermost in his mind he said, "Cobbett must have run mad to leave such a large sum in the house. He might as well advertise for someone to come and steal it."

Sarah's eyes gleamed with mischief. "Indeed he might."

"Wait . . . now wait a minute." George's mind was racing. He had never expected to find a way out of his difficulties so soon. The speed with which this rather dubious channel of escape had opened up took his breath away. So desperate was his need, however, that he did not even consider the criminal aspects of the situation. He muttered, half to himself, "How could such a thing be accomplished?"

Sarah swung her legs off the sofa and leaned forward, fists clenched on her knees, eager as a child at the prospect

of an adventure to lighten the dull routine of her days. "If I can, I shall contrive to leave a window open when we go out. There is little hope of putting a door on the latch I fear." She giggled nervously. "Mr Cobbett is constantly upon the alert for burglars, but I may be able to unscrew one of the window catches without his suspecting. The one in the back kitchen will suit I think. I can set a pot of flowers upon the sill to conceal my tampering."

Her eyes shone with excitement as she went on, "If I am successful I shall take Thomas for his walk on Tuesday morning and leave a note behind Patience's tombstone . . . you know, in the place where we used to hide our notes as children, and you may retrieve it later from there. It is too dangerous to send Lizzie over to Frinton Park with a letter, in case she is questioned afterwards by Mr Cobbett. We do not want him to make any connection with the Darker family."

Sarah was quite beside herself with her own cleverness, but George was looking doubtful. "It will take a bit of doing to squeeze myself through a cottage window, and if someone should see me forcing entry into the house when the family is known to be from home they might call up the constable."

Brother and sister talked on for another half hour, discussing and discarding ideas, polishing up their plan until no loopholes could be easily discerned. "Take everything that is in the chest," warned Sarah as George rose to go, and the sounds of young Thomas tuning up for his early evening feed could be heard through the open window. "If you leave so much as a groat behind the constable will wonder why."

"Ah, yes," George returned with a smile. "The constable. I must not forget about our worthy guardian of the law. There will be something of a hue and cry when Cobbett discovers the loss of his money I should judge."

"I should not be surprised if he were to summon the red-coats from Hollingbury camp," laughed Sarah.

George commented ruefully, "There will not be much left of your dowry after I have settled accounts with that greedy little whore in Brighton."

"Will you please to keep the remaining thousand pounds safe for me, George? As soon as Thomas is grown bigger I shall go to London. The money will give me a good start."

"I shall open an account for you with Messrs. Paxton and Company of Pall Mall the very next time I go to London," he promised. "Let us say under the name of Cawley . . . Cowley, or some such, so that you will not be put to the necessity of altering the initials on your bridal trunks. If you leave the money there for a twelvemonth the bank will pay you interest at the rate of five per cent per annum. I shall require a signature from you, of course, but we can settle all such details later. First we must secure the prize."

As he mounted his horse George heard the clang of the school bell heralding the call to freedom. He walked "Templar" through to the back garden of the cottage, passed through the little wicket gate into the lane which separated the school-house and the cottage from the churchyard, and was out of sight before Mr Sidney Cobbett emerged with his flock.

The robbery at the school-master's house caused quite a sensation in Piddingfold village. Mr Cobbett, being of the opinion that the Piddingfold constable could not solve the mystery single-handed, a second constable was sent for from Newporth and yet a third from Lewes, and various known vagrants were rounded up and questioned. None of those arrested could justifiably be held upon the flimsy evidence available, and all were allowed to go free.

Sarah dealt coolly and calmly with the questions put to her by the officers of the law, who treated her with the utmost respect and could not hide their embarrassment at having to interrogate a lady. After ascertaining that she had seen no suspicious characters hanging round the

cottage on the day before the robbery, and upon receiving her assurance that the servants were honest, they took their departure and repaired to the "Blue Boar" to see if the landlord of that hostelry had any ideas. Six pints of ale later they were no further forward with their investigations.

As for Mr Sidney Cobbett, he had questions of his own to put to his wife. Determinedly attacking Cook's apology for a rabbit pie, thinly disguised as a venison pasty—"I can't do nothing without the proper vittles, sir"—he inquired if Sarah had spoken of the gold to anyone outside the immediate family. "For I know very well, my dear, that you are unable to resist engaging all and sundry in conversation at the monthly assemblies. It will not be long before you gain the unenviable reputation of being the village gossip."

"I am not in the habit," countered she steadily, "of discussing my private affairs with mere acquaintances. Had you experienced the good fortune to be raised as a gentleman you would know perfectly well that a lady, especially one of high standing in the county, is required to speak to as many people as possible upon social occasions. It is quite apparent to me, sir, that you cannot distinguish the difference between polite social intercourse and mere gossip. You are to be pitied for your want of education."

This contemptuous reply produced a dusky red flush which slowly dyed Mr Cobbett's cheeks crimson and made him look like a schoolboy who has been accused of some unspeakable offence. "No, ma'am, I am not a gentleman," said he tightly, "and you forfeited your right to be called a lady when you foisted your bastard upon me!"

It was the first time that he had ever given her any indication that he believed their child had been fathered by another man. He watched her closely as she sullenly picked at her food, but he did not refer to the matter again. Her refusal to deny his accusation had merely confirmed his hardening suspicions that she had deceived him over the matter of the [illegible] doubtful paternity did not seem to Sarah to cause him as much concern as the loss of his money. "You told no one of the money, no one at all?"

"No!" she almost shrieked the word at him. "Pray, do not ask me that question again. I have answered a thousand times . . . no!"

His harsh voice, with its hint of a whine, played upon her taut nerves. But he was not to be put off by her manifest reluctance to help him over the recovery of his money. "You see, my dear Sarah, contrary to the opinion of the constables, I simply do not believe that the thief was some stray vagabond. The lock of my chest was neatly picked, not wrenched open as one would expect a passing vagrant to do. The man who robbed me appears to have been a professional at his trade, and why, I keep asking myself, should a professional thief be attracted to my humble abode unless he had got wind that there was a large prize waiting to be seized?"

Primly, Sidney Cobbett put down his knife and fork and patted his lips with his napkin. She, meanwhile, observed him narrowly, wary as a cat, and afraid all at once that he would hit upon the truth. It had become plain to her that he would wrestle with the problem until he came to a satisfactory conclusion.

His next words proved the truth of this assumption. "Now, ma'am, let us begin at the beginning, if you please. Who, amongst the members of our respective families did you tell about the money?"

With lips pressed firmly over clenched teeth, eyes opaque with fury, she rose from the table and used Mama's old exucse. "Sir, I have a monstrous painful megrim. I am going to lie down."

"No, ma'am, you are not!" He sprang to his feet and before she could move he had rounded the table, seized her by the arm and was forcing her back into her chair. A hard slap across the cheek completed the discipline.

Outraged and tearful she rounded on him. "How dare you! How dare you strike me!"

"I dare, ma'am because, with all your fine arts and graces, you now have a husband whose chattel you have become." His stale breath fanned her cheek. "I have the right to keep you locked within doors if you do not obey me."

The roughness of his manner frightened her. She thought he looked a little mad, and rightly attributed the change in him to the loss of his cherished money. He had never thought ever to possess so much, and to have it filched from under his very nose was enough to throw him into a state of panic bordering on dementia. The brightness of his eyes and the savagely down-turned mouth advised her that the best course would be to humour him. She forced herself to relax, and sensing her submission he let go of her arm. "That is better. Now we can get on." He returned to his chair and very deliberately repeated his last question.

She thought for a moment before replying and decided to change her tune. No harm would be done by admitting that she had told Papa. "I told Papa because I was worried about the money being in the house, and he said you ought to put it in the bank." In fact, Papa had shown very little interest in the matter. That once loving face had turned to unforgiving stone, for James Darker had shut his daughter out of his life, and when she had ventured to complain of her husband's tight-fistedness he had said curtly, "If you have nothing you cannot afford to be extravagant."

"Did you tell anyone else?"

There was no harm either—though this time it was an outright lie—in professing to have told Mama and Aunt Amelia and Uncle Robert. The more the merrier. It would give Cobbett plenty to think about. She proceeded to list them all, one by one, ticking them off on her fingers and watching his face go sour. "The polite social intercourse of a lady?" he sneered. The gibe only made her smile.

"Well, that proves my point," he was saying bitterly. "The world and his wife knows." He went on, sounding brisk and business-like. "You will oblige me by visiting all those to whom you have so rashly communicated this private intelligence, and you will ask each and every one if they have passed on the information to another living soul. I can then make a list and pursue my inquiries further."

His earnestness made her want to laugh, but her face still smarted from the slap he had administered, and she hated him for his dominance over her. She consoled herself with the thought that she was the richer by one thousand pounds at his expense, and inquired blandly, "With whom shall I begin?"

He pondered this question for a moment as he rolled a sip of George's madeira round his unappreciative tongue and plumped for Aunt Amelia. "Then we may learn how many ailing villagers have departed from your Uncle Robert's dispensary agog with the knowledge that the village schoolmaster has a fortune in gold in his guest bedroom."

Sheer curiosity prompted her to ask, "How far do you intend to carry this investigation?"

His response was sharp. "Until I have satisfied myself that further inquiries would be pointless."

She gave a disinterested shrug. "For my part I do not think it is worth the effort. It will turn out to be a wild-goose chase. The thief is well away by now."

He pushed back his chair and rose to his feet. "Nevertheless, I shall do all within my power to apprehend the criminal and bring him to justice."

George went to see Emily Pinkerton in her basement room in North Street. She smiled her thanks as he placed a weighty leather drawstring bag on the table. "Are you not bursting with eagerness to count it?" A sardonic lift of one eyebrow accompanied the question. Her smile broadened. "You wouldn' cheat me, Georgie."

Turning his back on her he made for the door and

would have departed without another word, but she called him back. "Georgie!" His head swivelled round. Emily jerked her thumb at the bag of money. "It ain't enough. I need another thousand for things I hadn' bargained for."

Slowly he walked back towards her and sat down. A dispirited look was directed at his tormentress. "What put such a conveniently round sum into that greedy head of yours?"

She giggled. "Bad luck for you, Georgie, that I can read. The papers was quite full of that robbery over at Piddin'-fold. School-master's place wasn' it? Him as is married to Miss Sarah Darker as was? Just over three-and-a-half thousand pounds was took accordin' to the 'Courier'."

Emily knew that she had forfeited George Darker's regard for ever and deliberately injected a hard note into her voice. "I want that other thousand, Georgie. I asked for too little in the beginnin'. I hadn' got things worked out proper then."

"And you have now?" he asked sarcastically. "You have definitely decided just how much you are going to milk me for in return for your silence?"

"You said it, Georgie."

He gave her a long, appraising stare. "I will bring it tomorrow. It is all I have got, so if you want more do not come to me. Just do your worst and tell Lucy the truth, and while you are at it, you might as well blow the gaff about the robbery . . . *and be damned to you!*"

The corners of her mouth lifted into a satisfied cat-smile. "Well, well, you are pickin' up the lingo. "Blow the gaff" indeed! As if I would! You won' hear no more from me, Georgie."

At this he gave a disbelieving grunt and was gone before she could carry out her intention to invite him to become a customer at her new place of business in West Street.

Sarah took the news of the loss of her money with remarkable stoicism. "We shall simply have to plan another robbery, George," said she in a tone of brisk efficiency. "Next time we can do it together."

OCTOBER, 1814

Sarah and George make plans and Miss Pinkerton repays her debt

During the next three months George and Sarah Darker successfully planned and carried out fifteen robberies, amassing almost four thousand pounds in bills and thirteen thousand pounds' worth of jewellery. George fenced some of the jewellery in London, having obtained a valuable connection in Seven Dials through the good offices of Miss Emily Pinkerton, at whose glossy red, gold and glass establishment he had now become a regular customer. The cash he obtained for the jewellery was deposited in Paxton and Company's bank. Pending disposal George and Sarah secreted their ill-gotten gains in the Darker family mausoleum, which was situated near the southern boundary of the park. George had had the key of the mausoleum copied in Lewes and now went about with the duplicate permanently lodged in the pocket of his pantaloons. Inside the mausoleum the notes and jewels were cached in a brass-bound leather box which had once contained church vestments, and which now afforded George and Sarah a convenient hiding-place for the proceeds of their nefarious activities.

Considerable changes had taken place in the two youngest Darker triplets since they had embarked upon their illegal enterprises three short months ago. To the world at large they presented familiar, recognisable faces, spoke polite, conventional words, observed the rules laid down by a wealthy society and were not conspicuous by their behaviour. They were both careful to maintain a reasonably even relationship with their respective spouses, George pandering to Lucy's whims and keeping her sweet with promises and gifts, and Sarah playing the role of the obedient wife, so that Mr Cobbett began to congratulate himself upon having asserted his superiority over a mere female, and a lady at that. Mr Cobbett was pleased to imagine that his wife was less reluctant to accept his advances in bed, although there were many occasions of late when he fell asleep as soon as his head touched the pillow. With wifely solicitude Sarah always insisted that he take a drink of hot chocolate before retiring, a beverage which, dangerously laced with laudanum, turned out to be remarkably soothing.

So they were careful, Sarah and George, to keep those about them in a state of comfortable complacency, and if Lucy nagged and Mr Cobbett waxed sarcastic about the gentry, neither was able to provoke the bitter quarrels which had once flared up all too easily between husband and wife. Those who gazed upon Sarah and George gazed upon the face of deception, a well-assumed mask which disguised the growing avarice and the almost complete absorption with self which brooked no interference from any outside source.

In repose their faces, so uncannily alike, were stiff and calculating, the eyes ever on the alert for signs of suspicion in others, and each began to develop a hard inner core of megalomania which was all the more dangerous because it was so well concealed. The transition from quite ordinary young people, neither wholly good nor wholly bad, into creatures devoted to the attainment of wealth by illegal means had been slow, and they themselves were not aware of the dramatic changes taking place within. Neither could have said, "A year ago I was a good sort of person and now I am given over to evil." Both would have claimed that adverse circumstances had forced them into doing that which would have been abhorrent to ordinary, decent people.

Fifteen houses in the county had suffered from their depredations during the last quarter of a year, the houses of family friends, where they had been welcomed as guests and had left as thieves in the night, where it had been all too easy to comb the upper rooms while the company made merry below. Inevitably, servants had been blamed for the ravages of George and Sarah, and accusations and dismissals had abounded, though nothing had actually been proved against the army of parlour-maids, footmen, cooks, grooms, boot-boys and skivvys who departed from the houses of the great bearing heavy grudges in their hearts and with their worldy goods bundled into wicker baskets.

At first there had been very little risk involved in pocketing a fistful of coins here and a carelessly abandoned trinket there, but an element of excitement had begun to creep in when George had picked the lock of young Mrs Lambton's jewellery case while Sarah stood on guard outside the bedroom door, quite prepared to swoon or throw a fit, whichever diversionary tactic seemed the most likely to prove effective in preventing discovery.

From then on nothing was worth trying unless the danger factor was present. As Sarah said, "We might as well combine business with pleasure." George wholeheartedly agreed. He had experienced a certain amount of sexual stimulation in cutting things really fine, and it was this spur to eroticism which had first sent him to Emily Pinkerton's new establishment in Brighton. Emily had been only too delighted to renew her acquaintance with George Darker upon a friendly footing, and even more ecstatic when she learned that he had taken to crime in earnest. She had remarked with her usual mischievous candour, "Well, I never thought you 'ad . . . had it in you, Georgie. It's a bloody marvel what a naggin' female can do to a man. Mrs Lucy drove you to it, thass it, innit, Georgie?"

Not a little indignation had been included in George's vehement disagreement with this outlandish point of view.

It was all very well for Miss Emily Pinkerton to make sly jokes at his expense when she alone was responsible for charting his unorthodox course.

Sarah also experienced the same highly-charged feelings which affected her brother and would have liked, if the opportunity had presented itself, to have taken a lover. The risk, however, was too great, and she forbore even to think about such a thing. Details of any extra-marital activities on her part would quickly reach the ears of her husband, and she was not yet ready to discard that tiresome encumbrance. Very soon now she and George would have to move their sphere of operations to London where the pickings, together with the dangers, were that much greater. The people of the locality had been "good" to them, but were now on their guard against thieves, and there was little more to be had.

On a boisterous afternoon in October, with the yellowing leaves whirling about her head and a brittle brown carpet beneath her feet, Sarah walked up to Frinton Park, ostensibly to visit her mother—Mr Cobbett did not boast his own carriage—and made a detour through the churchyard. There she met her brother. There was nothing at all remarkable in this, and any passers-by, descrying brother and sister perched companionably alongside each other on the mossy churchyard wall, would have smiled and bowed, or touched a forelock and offered a respectful "Good-afternoon, sir . . . madam," according to kind.

Sarah bunched up her skirts to make a "cushion" against the cold stone of the wall, looked down at the grave of Patience Westlake—by common consent they always took up their stations beside the daisy-covered mound—and remarked, "She was arrested in the first place for stealing a pair of gloves. Her crime seems paltry by comparison with ours."

Her brother laughed. "Ah, well, she did go on to commit murder. If we are caught it is more than likely that transportation will be our lot, in which case we can start all over again in a new country."

Sarah took him seriously and argued, "But they do not set people free when they take them to Botany Bay. They are bought as slaves by the local farmers and land-owners, or made to work in factories."

"How very knowledgeable you are upon the subject of convicted felons."

She tugged at the long grasses which grew up to hug the dry stone wall. "I obtained that information from my revered spouse. He prepared a lesson for the children on the lives of English convicts in Australia."

"To serve as a deterrent to the taking up of a life of crime I suppose?"

Sarah made a noise of disgust. "Cobbett enjoys frightening them. He reads them horrid little stories about children who have died in torment because they disobeyed their mothers and fathers."

George snorted with laughter. "Children like us."

His sister chewed reflectively upon a piece of ribwort. "Have you ever thought about getting caught?"

"Not very much," he admitted. "If I have thought about it at all I have always imagined myself talking my way out of trouble."

"In Sussex perhaps," she agreed. "Who would believe that a son and daughter of the gentry stoop to such low practices? In London it would be different. If we go there I think we should arm ourselves. I should much rather die than be taken, and a pistol would hold off immediate pursuit."

He pursed his lips doubtfully, drummed his heels against the wall and reminded her, "Robbery with a deadly weapon carries the death penalty."

"They have got to catch us first."

His grin was admiring. "What a bold creature you have turned out to be."

"And shall be bolder," she boasted, "until I have

collected at least fifty thousand pounds. Then I shall retire from my life of crime and buy myself a fine house. I shall live in it with my lover."

"I think we should move on very soon now," George said, with a smile for his sister's aspirations. "Apart from anything else Lucy is driving me to distraction."

Sarah threw her brother a sharp look. "Then you had better purchase some pistols, for I shall not go to London without proper protection."

George was frowning. "We have not really thought this thing through you know. It is easy enough for us to steal from Papa's friends, but going to London is an entirely different kettle of fish."

His sister did not agree. "Aunt Augusta has a great many friends in London society to whom we may obtain introductions. They will be fair game."

"But is Aunt Augusta likely to approve of our having run away from home? If she does not she may refuse us permission to call on her."

"I shall get round her." Sarah sounded very confident. "She admires people with spirit, at least she has always professed to do so." A nudge directed her brother's attention to a figure on horseback. "There is Papa on 'Sultan'. I think he has seen us. We had better go up to the house, for I promised Mama that I would arrive exactly at four o'clock for tea."

The two jumped down from the wall and Sarah took her brother's arm. "Shall we stay in Piddingfold until after Christmas?"

He nodded. "Meanwhile, I intend to carry out one more little enterprise."

"Where?" Sharp curiosity invaded her features.

A slow smile spread across George's face. "At Miss Emily Pinkerton's new whore-house in West Street."

Emily Pinkerton compared the statement from the bank with her written accounts and found all correct to the last farthing. It was a great relief to her that the bank had now assumed the responsibility for looking after her money, which she had previously kept in a tin box under her bed. She had not been in business three months before the tin box had become too small to hold all the silver pieces which had been transferred from the sticky palms of prurient gentlemen into her own dainty paw after the satisfactory conclusion of a "contract".

Emily liked to think of her transactions as "contracts", a convenient euphemism to give the whole thing an air of solid respectability. Respectability meant a great deal to Emily. It was what she had craved during the whole of her short life. She was now a remarkably mature eighteen-year-old, and the wind was set fair for a happy and comfortable future. That she had acquired her start in life through foul means was a thing not often thought about by Emily. When she did have time to think about George Darker's money it was with a sense of having properly avenged herself upon a man who had served her an extremely bad turn. There was even a measure of virtue about making a man pay for his perfidy, for having taken advantage of a weak, innocent girl who had done her level best to please him.

Emily's dreams for the future were rosy. She visualized a house in London and a country retreat, perhaps in the heart of Surrey, not more than an hour's carriage drive from London. Both her houses would be staffed by competent servants who would supply her every need, and she would keep dogs and riding horses, and order Earl Grey's China tea from Batherton's in Oxford Street. No masculine figure inhabited Emily's day-dreams, for she had long since reached the conclusion that men were the cause of most of the troubles in this world, and that the earth would be a better place without them.

A female servant knocked on the door and came in to inform Madam that Mr Francis Darker had arrived and wished to see her. Emily quickly gathered up her papers—

it would never do for George to see how much per month was paid into the Sussex Penny Bank at Brighton—and thrust them into the drawer of her desk. She locked the drawer and put the key, with others, into the pocket of her expensive green merino dress, a dress which she had had made up because she thought it gave her the air of an efficient house-keeper.

George came in, closing the door behind him. She smiled easily up at him and indicated a chair. "Good-evening, George. Have you come to make a contract?"

The accent was so very nearly that of a real lady that George felt like laughing out loud. He managed to keep a sober countenance, however, and after returning her greeting with grave politeness, sat down, very much at ease now in her presence. It seemed that he had altogether forgiven her venture into the realms of extortion. "My dear Emily, your two young ladies, Geraldine and Amy are their names I believe, have already accosted me in the hall, and have begged me to contract for them, so how could I possibly refuse, especially since they are trying to enlist my sympathy for certain quite violent bruises, sustained, I am given to understand, at the hands of a drunken sea-dog."

Emily frowned and made a genteel noise of distress. "Yes, that was most unfortunate, to say the least, and those two are making a great deal of noise about the incident. I may have to dispense with their services if they cannot be persuaded to control themselves and hold their tongues." By way of explanation she went on, and now he was hard put to it to suppress a smile at her prim delivery, "The personage in question did not appear to be in his cups when he was admitted to the house, but he did have a bottle with him, and I suppose was simply able to carry his liquor well enough to deceive me. He went berserk, as they say, and there was nearly murder done."

"How very trying for you," George said. He might have been commiserating with a mother complaining about recalcitrant children. Was he mocking her, wondered

Emily? She could never be sure with George these days. He had changed very much since the old days in North Street. She said in business-like tones, "A guinea each for the hour, or thirty shillings if you take them both together."

He gave the offer his earnest consideration and at length decided, "One at a time, if you please. I do not feel man enough this evening to engage them both at once."

"Very well."

Her cool efficiency never ceased to amaze him. Even when she was making the most sordid of bargains concerning perhaps some "special requirements", which, to the ears of the uninitiated sounded distinctly odd, she would put on an air of being about to supply some highly-priced commodity which only her establishment could be relied upon to deliver in mint condition. She was quite outrageous. She would be more than a little indignant when she discovered what he had really come for. First, however, he would enjoy himself. His little trap could be sprung later, when Emily was less alert, a trifle more exhausted at the end of a long night.

Something over three hours went by before George emerged from his labours, wondering ruefully if he should have abstained from such frolics when the real business in hand had not yet been attempted. A quick swig from his pocket-flask of brandy revived him, and with silent tread he descended the stairs to the hall. A light shining from beneath Emily's door signified that the lady of the house was still working. George permitted himself a grin as he thought of all that money to be had for the taking. She was sure to keep it in what she was pleased to call her office. In the wall cupboard? Under the desk? It would not take him long to smoke it out.

He went boldly in, without knocking, and came upon Emily seated at her desk and engrossed in earnest conversation with a flashily dressed young gentleman who sat very close to her and seemed to be putting forward some sort of proposition. The young gentleman was obviously eager to please. Emily looked up, fuming with annoyance at the interruption. "Should you not have knocked, Mr Darker?"

That was rich, being taught his manners by a back-street slut. George swallowed a hoot of laughter and apologised. How to get rid of the young man?

"Could I speak with you for a moment?"

"Well, what is it?"

His eyes swivelled significantly to take in the presence of the third party, and she said impatiently, "It cannot be all that private. Besides, Mr Lucas and I are going into business together. There will be no secrets between us."

Mr Lucas looked extraordinarily gratified at this positive statement. He had not been absolutely sure that he had captured Miss Pinkerton's interest in his scheme to open a chain of palaces of pleasure all along the South Coast before this idiot of a fellow had barged in and spoiled his train of thought.

It seemed to George that the stares directed at him were less than friendly. He tried again. "Emily, if you *please*. You know I would not ask unless it was important."

"You shouldn'a come in without knocking," the young woman said stonily, dropping the mask of ladylike gentility. "You take advantage, you do. Now say what you got to say and get out. I'm busy."

Very slowly George's hand went to the inside pocket of his frock-coat. From it he withdrew a gleaming silver pistol; with a hand as steady as a rock he pointed it directly at Emily. The startled Mr Lucas leapt to his feet as if he had been stung, made as if to spring at George, hesitated foolishly and slumped back into his chair.

Emily stared levelly at the pistol and inquired coolly, "Is it money you're after, Mr Darker?"

"Perceptive of you, Miss Pinkerton."

"Started robbin' yer own now, 'ave you?" The contemptuous expression on her face, combined with the sudden loss of precise formality in her speech, sent the laughter bubbling up from his chest. "I only want the return of my loan. It *was* a loan, was it not?"

She cut short these fancy fencing tactics with "I doan keep no money 'ere, Frankie. All my takings is in the bank."

For a moment he did not believe her until she added, "You know me, Frankie. I doan take no chances."

He did know her, and her statement put him momentarily at a loss, while he marvelled at her coolness under stress. She was still remembering to call him by his brother's name in front of a third party. Quick to notice his hesitation, her small cat mouth turned up in a smug, gratified smile. "If that thing goes off, Frankie, you'll bring all my girls on the trot, along with their gentlemen friends, who won't like being interrupted in what they're doing."

The truth of this statement was indisputable, but he had shown his hand now, and this was a situation from which he must extricate himself with the utmost possible despatch. There were no pickings to be had, and he had blundered badly. His first mistake had been in supposing that Emily kept her takings on the premises—he should have remembered her forthright views about "'avin' lump sums in the 'ouse"—and his second that she would be alone when he began to put his plan into operation. He backed towards the door and without looking round turned the key in the lock.

Emily's eyes flickered backwards and forwards uneasily between the door and George, and widened in genuine alarm as the pistol was fractionally lowered and more accurately aimed at her heart. But she was still not convinced that he meant to kill her, not her Georgie, who had been such a jolly good chum in days gone by, who had loved her and teased her and promised to buy her a dog . . . "Ow, doan be a bloody fool. You'n me, Georgie, we. . . ." The pistol exploded with an ear-shattering report, accompanied by a high-pitched scream from Mr

Lucas, who jumped to his feet and clung to the desk for support. George was on him in a flash, dealing him a savage blow on the head. As he keeled over and collapsed in a heap on the floor Mr Lucas made no sound other than a low, defeated sigh.

The crumpled figure of Emily Pinkerton, face down, was sprawled across the desk, inanimate as a stuffed doll. blood oozed from a hole in her forehead. With a sweep of his arm George overthrew the paraffin lamp, the sole source of light in the room, and made for the window. Wrenching up the sash he flung his leg over the sill, a single backward glance satisfying him that the room would shortly be a blazing inferno.

He knew the house well. It was situated at the end of a terrace, with an alley giving access to the back garden. He raced round to the rear and re-entered the house by the dining-room window. Two candles burned feebly on a table littered with the remains of the evening meal. As he blundered his way to the door George realised that he was still holding the smoking pistol. He stuffed it back into his pocket. Cautiously he eased back the door-catch. People were tumbling down the stairs and into the front hall, and no one observed George as he came out of the dining-room to join the throng gathering about Emily's office door.

Puffs of black smoke swirled upwards from under the bottom of the door. Someone called for an axe, but minutes passed before it was brought, and when the door was finally smashed in the watchers were forced back by the leaping tongues of flame and billows of dense smoke which rolled forth into the hall. In the general confusion George made his escape.

The next day the "Brighton Courier" carried the story of the fire which had taken place in a house of ill-repute in West Street. Two bodies had been discovered, one of which was believed to be that of Miss Emily Pinkerton, the proprietress of that unholy establishment. The other was that of an unidentifiable male. Observation revealed the fact that the female had been shot in the head, and it was suspected that the two might have been the victims of a dissatisfied client. The only clue left behind by the murderer was a gentleman's gold half-hunter watch, an everyday object which bore no mark of its owner's identity. The mystery was likely to prove difficult of solution since gentlemen visiting the house were not in the habit of supplying their correct names or places of residence.

At Frinton Park Lucy studied the "Courier" and thought it a marvellous coincidence that the name of the murdered woman should be the same as that of the respectable milliner who had come to see her mother-in-law.

NOVEMBER, 1814

George and Sarah make plans and James Darker is pleasantly surprised

George and Sarah had now determined upon leaving Piddingfold, with all its restrictions and impediments to their enterprises, for the gold-paved streets of London town, deeming it prudent to secure for themselves a house in the metropolis before the beginning of the new season, when accommodation would be at a premium. They now had in their possession seven thousand pounds in bills and a small quantity of jewels still waiting to be fenced. This was in addition to the money safely stashed away in Paxton's bank. Sarah declared with a pout that she would not be seen dead in London in her present shabby clothes, but George persuaded her that they must travel as light as possible, and that the London shops would offer a great deal more variety of choice than those in the Brighton Lanes, fashionable as these last had become.

"We could go before Christmas," George said, "but we shall be twenty-one on the twenty-seventh of December and Papa is sure to give us the traditional coming-of-age gratuities. Five hundred pounds for Francis and me and two hundred and fifty pounds for you. It will be worth waiting for a few days longer."

Sarah agreed that this would be the best course. "We might as well collect everything we can. It will take us a while to settle down, and our expenses in London will be considerable."

George asked, "Shall we present ourselves to the world as brother and sister, or as husband and wife?"

She took a moment or two to think about this, weighing up the pros and cons, but at length said positively, "Brother and sister it must be if we are to enlist the aid of Aunt Augusta in introducing us to society. She would never agree to our sailing under false colours." A sly smile played at the corners of her mouth. "Besides, I should so much dislike to be the cause of inhibiting your affairs of the heart, George. A wife would be a great burden in that direction you know."

"We must not embark upon anything in the way of permanent liaisons. Shall you be able to stop yourself from forming an attachment, Sarah?" George was remembering Captain Millars, who, despite the living evidence of his son, had become such a nebulous, unremarkable figure in their lives.

"I cannot absolutely guarantee to remain heart-whole," she admitted candidly, "but if my affections should become seriously engaged I shall abandon our partnership and retire, and my future husband will think that I am a woman of property."

"You would commit bigamy?"

She looked truly amazed. "Indeed, I had not thought of that. I have never regarded Mr Cobbett as my true husband."

"You cannot dismiss him so easily," George warned her. "You are bound together by the ties of the church and of the law, and may not be parted without a wealth of legal acrobatics. An action for criminal conversation has to be brought before a jury, and after that the matter must be settled by a Bill to be decided upon in the House of Lords."

Seeing her downcast looks he attempted to cheer her. "It is fruitless and unprofitable to cross our bridges before we come to them. The whole of our lives are yet to be lived, to be *enjoyed*, so let us not worry about the obstacles which will certainly bestrew our paths."

Sarah laughed gaily. "Why, George, you are become something of a philosopher!"

On an exceptionally mild night in early November, with the thermometer in the stables registering fifty degrees Fahrenheit, James Darker donned his heavy caped overcoat over his night-shirt, and taking a dark-lantern from the rack in the kitchen, went for a walk in the park. Claudine, fast asleep in the great four-poster, did not stir, and there were no sounds coming from the adjoining bedroom to suggest that old William was wakeful.

The nocturnal wanderer, having made his way along the carpeted passage, ascertaining as he did so that no light shone from beneath the firmly closed door behind which he supposed that Francis and Lucy might be making half-hearted efforts to beget an heir for Frinton Park, sighed as he thought about that ill-matched pair, and vowed that his youngest son, when he returned from the wars, should be persuaded to marry "out of the family". Not that George would need much persuading when faced with the example of Francis and Lucy.

It was half-past one in the morning. The air which fanned James's face as he opened the front door could almost be described as balmy. It seemed that the seasons had turned topsy-turvy and that this must surely be spring. Descending the balustraded stone steps of his father's imposing residence, James crunched his way over the gravelled sweep towards the lawn. His unstockinged legs and feet felt slightly uncomfortable in the leather boots which he had hastily donned.

James had been rendered restless by the mulling over of a problem concerning his own future and that of his immediate family. The past two years had been full of problems, mainly in connection with money, and the strain of maintaining such a large property grew greater by the month. He had succeeded, thank God, in keeping his head above water, aided by two good harvests in succession, and although he had very little capital to call upon it was enough to tide him over a couple of bad years. There were a number of repairs required in the house, but those would have to wait until the capital in the bank had at least doubled. By one means and one means only could this desirable state of affairs be brought about, a means which would necessitate the immediate expenditure of some of the existing capital which James liked to keep in reserve. What he had to decide, very soon, was whether or not he should take a gamble.

The idea had been suggested to him seven months ago by his friend, Lord Frederick Oliver, into whose alert and receptive ear had lately been delivered the intelligence that the Member of Parliament for Brighton, a dropsical gentleman who was now putting a severe strain upon the springs of his carriage and an equally severe strain upon the hearts of his horses as they pulled him uphill, was about to apply for the Chiltern Hundreds. The vacant seat could, in the well-informed opinion of Lord Frederick, be purchased for the sum of around ten thousand pounds. This amount, or something akin to it, would need to be distributed among voters and public officials alike if the seat was to be secured.

"Contacts, my dear fellow, are what you so urgently require," Lord Frederick had said with his charmingly frank air. You are buried alive in the wilds of Sussex, like a yeoman farmer contemplating his milk yields and rotating his dashed crops, until your brain is so addled by it all that you can scarcely remember what day of the week it is." Lord Frederick had waved his long, thin arms in a broadly expansive gesture. "Put yourself in the halls of power, dear fellow, and there is no knowing to what heights you may attain by the judicious use of your ears and eyes."

James had been vastly amused, and at the same time very curious to know what these cryptic references to contacts might mean. He made bold to ask. "What is the exact nature of these contacts you are pleased to rattle on so knowledgeably about, Fred?" Lord Frederick had laid a finger alongside his bony, pointed nose. "Ah! I was wondering when you were going to trot out your bump of curiosity, dear fellow. There is one gentleman in particular whom I have in mind as peculiarly suited to meet the needs of your case. Mr Belding is his name. He is the Member for East London and has recently purchased a sugar plantation in Jamaica. The word is out that he is looking for a partner in this enterprise. When I heard about it I was struck most forcibly by the notion that the Darker family having been associated with the slave-trade for so many years must know a great deal about the buying and selling of blacks, and of the manner in which these plantations are run. I believe that your Papa has made several trips to the West Indies on his own slavers?"

That was true, and Papa had kept detailed records of all the voyages undertaken by his three ships, and of the slaves bought and sold. William Darker had preferred to direct his unflagging energies towards the supplying of cheap labour in his native England, but there was little he did not know about the day-to-day running of a sugar plantation. As a boy James had listened to numerous stories about sugar-planters from his father's own lips.

"The West Indian planter," Lord Frederick had pursued carelessly, "is not a sentimentalist, dear fellow. If my information is correct they operate on the principle that it is cheaper to work a slave to death and buy a new one than to wait for him to replenish his numbers naturally. Ergo, the slaves are worked to death. That is where your good offices would come in. A little picking of old Mr Darker's brains and you will know all there is to know about where to go for the best and strongest specimens, what to charge for them, how to breed to produce the best stock, etcetera. The slave-trade may be done for in England, dear fellow, but it flourishes like the green bay tree on distant shores."

James's enthusiasm and interest had been captured by his friend's words, and his previous young man's notions concerning the evil inherent in trading in human flesh, inculcated into him by his mother, quickly deserted him under the pressure of impending financial disaster. Pecuniary interests must come first. It was a question of the survival of the fittest. "Do you think it possible that I may salvage our ships?" he had asked eagerly.

Lord Frederick had had no doubts on that score. "I can get them towed down to Buckler's Hard and re-fitted for you for less than nothing," he had assured James. "Lord Montagu is a friend of my father's," and as James had continued to look doubtful, patently totting up the enormous expenses he would incur if he embarked upon this evidently costly enterprise, "You will be able to borrow capital from Coutt's bank, and perhaps even form a joint-stock company to bolster up funds and give yourself a good start. There is money in it, dear fellow, you may take my word upon that. Now that His Grace of Wellington is over the Pyrenees and into France there is talk that a peace will shortly be concluded with the Emperor Napoleon, but England has endured a long and costly war, and wars have to be paid for. Who pays?" Fred had inquired rhetorically, "Why, you and I do, dear fellow, with crippling taxes on our land, and possibly our incomes, from whatever source we may obtain the latter. Mr Vansittart may bleat away in the House about abolishing taxes as soon as the war is paid for, but do not believe a word of it. Once the government is on to a good thing like that they will keep a fast hold, like a terrier to a rat. Owners of estates like ours will be hard put to it to keep things going.

"Indeed," Fred had continued, "many of my friends are already selling up and buying houses in London from which they conduct their businesses. There is no room now for the dilettante farmer with one foot in the country and the other in the Stock Exchange in London. Times are changing, dear fellow, and if we do not change with them we shall find ourselves up to our necks in the mire of debts and foreclosures."

Fred had always had a persuasive way with him. Add to that the fact that he spoke good, sound commonsense and James was very much inclined to take the plunge. It wanted only a few hours of good, hard thinking to sort out the details and take a final decision as to whether the thing was worth the risk he must inevitably take. There was too the possibility that George, who had so far had the good fortune to survive the Peninsular campaign, would find himself at a loose end now that the fighting had ceased. James rather fancied from the tone of his son's letters that a career in the army was only palatable to him if he were constantly required to use his sword. Gambling and drinking in the London clubs with fellow officers was not his style at all. He had to be up and doing, and he would probably make a good job of running a sugar plantation. James did not subscribe to Lord Frederick's view that one could own a plantation and leave it to be run by underlings who reported home once or twice a year. Absenteeism went against his notions of what was to be expected of a gentleman. With George on the spot, and himself running things from the London end, there was a fortune to be made for the man who was willing to take a chance.

The factor which finally decided James as he circumnavigated his estate on that November night, was that the ground he now trod upon would be preserved for future generations of Darkers to enjoy. This prompted yet another thought. It looked as though it would be left to George to produce an heir for Frinton Park, since Lucy still showed no signs of being fertile. James became filled with a sudden sense of urgency, a fierce desire to see his younger son home safe and sound.

He was about to enter the wilderness, an area of land which had been left to grow as it would with shrubs and trees—a perfect hide-and-seek playground for the family—when a light, flickering in and out among the clump of elm trees by the lake caught his attention. A firefly? No, too bright. As he stood, rooted to the spot, his eyes firmly fixed on the light, it moved a little to the right and was gone. James fought back a yawn. He had a sudden longing for his bed, for he felt now that he could sleep. His problem was on the way to becoming resolved. If it had not been for the fact that the light had shown itself in the vicinity of the mausoleum, the pull of sleep would have been too great to resist, but the thought that someone might be robbing his dead of their gold wedding-rings sent James off to investigate.

He covered the half-mile of parkland which separated him from the family's last resting-place in under ten minutes, and the hairs crawled on the back of his neck as he saw that the wrought-iron gate, set into the iron fence which enclosed the little garden, was swinging open on its hinges and faintly creaking in the light breeze. He negotiated the narrow brick path with caution and mounting the steps which fronted this rather pretentious structure, which had been modelled in the style of the Temple of Diana at Blenheim Palace, passed under the arcade of Doric columns and paused before the oaken door. It stood slightly ajar, and now he could hear the sound of voices coming from within. James looked about him for a possible weapon. The iron boot-scraper seemed to offer itself as his only means of protection. He picked it up and tentatively pushed the door inwards. Its well-oiled hinges made no sound.

Very slowly James inserted his head into the widening aperture. He could hear the voices more clearly now, distinguishing a word or two . . . ". . . worth at least a hundred pounds. . . ." "This one is too distinctive . . . broken up. . . ." It took a second or two for the familiarity of those tones to penetrate his consciousness. Then he stiffened as his daughter said disparagingly, "These stones are not fine enough to fetch much. It is hardly worth taking such a bauble with us," to which the voice of his son replied with a laugh, "George Lambton was always a miserly animal. His spouse has the most tawdry jewels in the county."

"Shall we leave it then?"

"By no means. We shall need every penny we can raise if we are to go to London."

James, his heart beating more rapidly than usual, his brain in a whirl, edged round the door and on silent feet retreated behind one of the pillars which circled the entire building and formed a sort of walkway round the perimeter. The narrow recess behind the pillars was furnished with seats of padded leather to accommodate funeral guests, and the gloom therein was so deep that James could creep yet closer to his children and still remain unobserved.

A lantern, placed strategically on the floor beside the malefactors, illuminated their well-known features and disclosed to their father's astonished gaze the old vestment chest, the lid of which was thrown back. Various articles were being extracted from the chest and re-stowed into a sack. With an almost audible gasp, which he managed to smother just in time, James recognised Lady Oliver's ruby necklace, the loss of which she had sincerely mourned, since it had been Fred's wedding-gift to her. There could be no doubt of it—and the impact of the sudden knowledge was truly shattering to the emotions—the mysterious thieves who had been invading the houses of the district for the past few months were clearly identified as his own children!

It all fitted neatly into place now that his bewildered brain began to sort it out. Francis's frequent absences from home, his unwillingness to take part in the day-to-day running of the estate, his grudging performance of routine tasks which he had previously carried out without a murmur of protest. Then there were the one or two unsatisfactorily explained visits to London, ostensibly to purchase new clothes. Had Francis been disposing of stolen property on these occasions? And his daughter too was involved in this hideous enterprise. How was it possible that flesh of his flesh could turn to such wickedness?

James, even had it been explained to him, would have

been unable to grasp that what had started out as a harmless-seeming prank had turned sour, corrupting the participants and leading them into performing acts of which they had never believed themselves capable. He was still in the throes of that initial, brutal shock at finding himself the progenitor of common thieves when he received a second, more stunning blow as Sarah asked, "George, where shall you hide the sack pending our departure?"

George? *George?* Great heavens, was it possible that this son of his was an imposter as well as a thief? Was it his heir who was fighting on the battle-grounds of Europe, risking his neck and the breaking of the direct Darker line, while his youngest son calmly assumed his brother's identity and actually married the bride intended for another?

James's whole body was consumed by a most terrifying rage. It burned up from his toes, coursed through his legs and loins, churned in his belly and penetrated his heart with the agonising slowness of a blunt knife. All his children had deceived him, all his thrice-cursed brood, who—he realised it now that it was too late—had rebelled against their chosen destinies from the very first. Francis, with his urge to carry a sword, Sarah with her irrational dislike of poor Dodgson Oliver, George with his cow eyes directed at Lucy and his reluctance to become a soldier. Ungrateful, odious progeny!

Swiftly and silently James regained the door, was through it in a trice, and with an arm strenghtened by rage, had slammed it shut. The conspirators had been careless enough to leave the key on the outside of the door and James turned it in the lock with a savage click. He fairly ran back to the house, and for the remainder of the night lay wakeful on his bed, devoting himself to thought. Of one thing he was quite certain. He would teach his children a lesson they would not quickly forget.

"It must have been Jack Gander," George said, naming his father's Head Groom. "He often prowls about the place at night, on the look-out for poachers. I suppose he noticed that the door was open and simply shut it."

"Slammed it," Sarah corrected, "*and* turned the key in the lock." She sounded very frightened and persisted, "Why should he slam it like that? And why did he pay no heed to our cries? He *must* have heard us."

This was a point which had been puzzling George, but he did not wish to alarm his sister too much, so he brushed her fears aside with a brisk invitation to her to "Come along, sister. Let us see how we are to get out of here."

A glance at the beautiful stained-glass windows, set high in the walls of the octagon, convinced him that there was no possible means by which they could gain egress there, but it might just be possible to hurl a chalice or a candlestick at one of the windows, in the hope that someone outside would notice the damage and come inside to investigate. The small altar boasted two heavy silver candlesticks, a silver vase, a gold crucifix on a stand and a gold chalice, all of which holy ornaments could be used for the purpose. But that was a last resort. The door was their best bet. It might be possible to force the lock.

Peering through the keyhole George was not surprised to see that the key had been removed. If it had been Jack who had locked them in he would have returned the key to its proper place in the house. In the event, the lock proved too sturdy to respond to his efforts with the knife which he always carried about his person for just such an emergency.

By this time the lantern was burning very low and would not afford light for longer than another half-hour. George judged it to be about five o'clock in the morning, and discovered to his annoyance that Francis's watch, which he still wore, had let him down. It registered a quarter past three and had stopped. Neither he nor Sarah had snatched so much as a wink of sleep. Their urgent need to escape, and the claustrophobic atmosphere of this macabre place, had kept them wakeful and alert as they racked their brains for some ingenious method by which they could regain their freedom.

Sarah sat down dispiritedly on one of the leather-covered benches and said tearfully, "We shall have to stay cooped up here until Mama comes to do the flowers on Friday. Oh, heavens, that is two days from now. We shall be desperately in want of food and water by then, and when we want to. . . ." Delicacy restrained her from completing the sentence, but George at once perceived her meaning. His own bladder was sending out urgent signals, and he would soon have no recourse but to relieve himself in a corner of the chapel. He reflected ruefully that it would be a somewhat harrowing experience for both of them to have to reveal the more animal sides of their natures.

Sarah indicated the floor with her forefinger and asked hesitantly, "Down there, in the vault. I suppose there is nothing which might be of any use to us?"

"The odd bone or two," he joked and was instantly made aware by his sister's reproachful looks that he had displayed a want of good taste which was not acceptable in their present circumstances. He mumbled an apology and gave himself up to thought. "Certainly there is no means down there by which we might regain our freedom. The walls are of solid brickwork." A sudden inspired gleam came into his cyc. "The biers? The coffins are laid upon wooden biers, bolted to the walls. If I could manage to prise one of those loose we could use it as a battering ram to break down the door. If we attack it at the weakest point, near the lock, it might give way. It is at least worth a try."

Her face registered alarm. "*I* could not go down. You will have to do it alone."

"I can manage," he assured her tersely. "Sheer desperation will give me the strength to do it."

"Do not. . . ." She faltered over her words, her face white as death. "Do not touch Grandmama. I could not bear to think of her being disturbed. She has such gentle eyes . . . in the portraits . . . you know."

He did not reply, but made his way instead to the trap-door which opened out on to a flight of steps leading to the vault below. His sister, he noted with grim cynicism, was no longer the arrogant, hard-eyed thief who had revelled in their joint, mad adventures. She had reverted to her original role of the dutiful daughter, a devil turned saint now that the cards were stacked against her. Women were like chameleons. They adapted to circumstances, changing their peacock colours to drab grey when concealment of their true natures was necessary. As he descended the stone steps into the dank, musty-smelling vault below George Darker prayed to his gods to give him strength.

"I must apologise for the absence of Mrs Darker," James Darker said pleasantly, eyeing his visitor with a certain amount of speculation. "She is suffering from a sore throat and has something of a fever. The physician has ordered her to stay in bed for a day or two."

Mr Cobbett offered his condolences, which even in James's preoccupied state of mind sounded half-hearted, and asked rather breathlessly, "You are of the opinion then that my wife will shortly return home?"

"I am, sir," returned James emphatically. "It is my belief that Sarah and my son Geo . . . Francis have taken it into their heads to go off on some jaunt, perhaps to Brighton, or even to London, and that they will return anon, shamefaced and full of apologies and excuses for their light behaviour." He engaged the other's eye with a look of great sobriety. "You must understand, sir, that my children have an excess of animal spirits which sometimes leads them into doing things which they afterwards very much regret. Rest assured that both shall be firmly taken to task by me upon their return."

"And by me, sir," responded Mr Cobbett bridling. Had Mr Darker forgotten that his daughter owed her sole duty to her husband now? "The whole thing is quite incredible," he continued in declamatory tones. "I am truly astonished that your daughter should have abandoned her husband and child in such a heartless fashion."

James permitted himself a small, tight smile—"your daughter" now that Sarah had committed the final, unforgiveable sin of temporary desertion, no longer "my wife". "If by that you are implying that I must attach the blame for her disappearance to myself," returned he icily, "then may I remind you, sir, that I merely gave you leave to call upon my daughter. I did not either assume or ask that you would propose marriage to her. That is a responsibility which you took upon your own shoulders. I cannot be called upon to answer for the conduct of a married woman. She has long been out of my sphere of influence."

The reprimand, along with the sudden change of tune, was received in silence. Only a tightening of the lips betrayed Mr Cobbett's seething anger. The school-master knew that he could never get the better of James Darker in a battle of words. "I shall make no attempt to find her," said he primly, giving a light shrug and assuming an air of studied nonchalance. "What if she does not return? Her son will do very well without such a mother."

James made a deprecatory gesture with his hands. "Come now, Cobbett. Let us not dramatize the situation. It is much too early to speak of abandonment. Should the runaways not return within three days I shall, of course, institute inquiries, and a search will be made for them. My son is still under age and I do have the guardianship of him until he is one and twenty."

The school-master digested this information in gloomy silence and sat staring at his father-in-law, who might have been forgiven for thinking that the uncomfortable interview was at an end. A gentleman, of course, would have known that it was time to take his leave. James coughed and half rose from his chair, a hint which only succeeded in provoking Mr Cobbett into unburdening his mind. "Sir," said he with a rush, "if my wife should not return, and we must not lose sight of the fact that such a possibility exists, I trust that I may rely upon you to provide adequately for your grandson. As you know, I am hardly in a position to. . . ."

Brusquely, James interrupted the tiresome pedagogue. "*Your* son, sir, must prove his worth before he receives any advancement from me. I shall, I trust, have other grandchildren. Each shall receive his or her due, provided that he or she proves to be a person imbued with a sense of duty."

Mr Cobbett felt it incumbent upon himself to remind Mr Darker that his eldest son, having apparently abandoned his wife, was unlikely ever to get her with child, and that his younger son, though presently sound in wind and limb, might at any moment fall prey to some foreign disease, or even meet his end upon the high seas in the very act of returning home. There was many a slip 'twixt the cup and the lip. In this sad eventuality, Mr Cobbett thought it entirely possible that young Thomas Cobbett might become the heir of Frinton Park.

James took the point, but could certainly not admit to the possibility of his children having gone off for good—he knew better. A sudden and most violent distaste for the presence of Sidney Cobbett in his house overcame him and he rose definitively to his feet, forcing the reluctant schoolmaster to do likewise. The latter turned away without offering his hand to his father-in-law and left the house in disgruntled silence.

After his guest had gone, striding across the park and cutting the air now and then with his walking-cane as if to say, "All this is very fine, but it does not impress *me*," James sat for a long time, motionless and wrapped in thought. Unlike his late visitor he knew that his son and daughter had not disappeared for ever, but it did occur to him that had he not chanced upon them in the mausoleum, to disappear was precisely what they had intended to do, and then the situation which Mr Cobbett had only too plainly spelled out, would have reared its head in earnest. Lucy would have remained childless and Francis might well have fallen victim to some unnameable disaster. The thought that Sarah's child might inherit Frinton Park was not to be borne.

James went to see his wife and was vaguely alarmed by the sight of her flushed cheeks and over-bright eyes. "How are you feeling, my dear?"

"Very hot," she complained. "My face is burning. Has Uncle Robert sent up my medicine?"

"Not yet," answered James. "It will be here directly." His voice was quiet and soothing.

"I shall not be able to change the flowers in the mausoleum on Friday," she fretted.

"I shall see to the flowers myself."

"Cannot Lucy do it?"

He shook his head and smiled briefly. "The place frightens her. She is convinced that it is haunted by the ghosts of the dead."

"Stupid creature," muttered Claudine. "She cannot please her husband because her tongue is as sharp as a razor, and now she complains because Francis has not been home all night. What a fuss about nothing. I told her that Francis is entitled to take his pleasure with a whore now and then, especially since she is not willing to play the part of a loving wife."

"Francis has gone off somewhere with Sarah," James said, registering disapproval. "I am very much afraid that they have gone to London and are presently engaged in some escapade or other, without giving a thought to the anxiety which you and I shall experience."

At first her eyes were disbelieving, an expression which quickly turned to anger. "It is her!" she accused, "that silly girl, with her demands for this and that, and her refusal to obey her husband. Oh, James, shall you not try to bring them back?"

James made a noise of disgust. "I shall give them three days in which to indulge their mischief, and then I shall institute a search for them. I do not believe that they will be long away. This is merely an attempt to defy me and assert some sort of independence. They shall very soon learn that independence is a luxury that they cannot well afford."

Claudine was crying now, and he became fearful lest this family "tragedy" retard her recovery. He said with the confidence born of secret knowledge, "You may take my word for it, my dear, that they will return, either today or tomorrow, feeling rather foolish and begging for our forgiveness."

An uncertain smile illuminated her pale features. "Do you truly think so? I hope very much that you are right . . . oh, heavens, how ill I feel . . . I should like to write to Aunt Augusta at Charlotte Street in case she has seen anything of them, but I do not think I am up to it. My head aches so. . . ."

"You must rest, my poor Claudine," he lectured her gravely. "I shall send Lucy up with your medicine as soon as it arrives. Now, please try to sleep. Sleep is such a great restorative."

The Wages of Sin

"We have been penned up here for six days," rasped George, peering at the marks he had made on the wall with his knife, a desecration of the work of an Italian master who had painstakingly fitted each little piece of coloured mosaic into a wonderfully lifelike portrait of the Virgin and Child. "We cannot last out much longer without water."

Sarah did not reply. She lay on the tiled floor, curled up like an animal, her breathing unusually light and shallow. For a moment George thought she was asleep, then she raised her head and stared at him listlessly, her pale eyes bright with the suspicion of a fever. "Have we drunk all the water in the vase?"

George's legs felt like lumps of lead as he moved over to the altar and picked up a silver vase, the only ornament which now remained in the mausoleum. The others had been hurled through the stained-glass windows, all to no effect. George had deliberately chosen the windows facing the park as the most likely to be detected by passers-by, but everyone at Frinton Park, family and servants alike, seemed to have been struck blind. "Almost empty," he announced, and replaced the vase on the altar. With a muttered curse he slumped down on to the floor, crossed his legs and lowered his head between his knees.

The two had now endured their captivity for six days without food, their only liquid intake having been the slimy greenish water contained in the silver flower vase. The fierce, stabbing pangs of hunger which had initially assailed them and had caused them to writhe in pain had, by this time, somewhat abated, and they had become used to the feeling of light-headedness produced by lack of nourishment. Being thirsty, they had quickly discovered, was by far the worst part of their ordeal. Flowers, dry and withered, lay scattered on the floor, and the water in the vase had been carefully rationed out, day by day. There was sufficient for one drink more each. "Why did not Mama come?" asked Sarah for the hundredth time, in that soft, whispery voice which was so unlike her normal, healthily musical tones. She shifted position, rolling over on to her back and flinging her arms above her head in a gesture of utter despair.

George's voice growled back. "She must have taken cold. I have never known her to neglect to replenish the flowers, not even when she had one of her headaches."

Slowly, painfully, Sarah sat up and slid towards her brother, propelling herself forward on her hands. She felt too weak to make the effort to pull herself upright, and the floor was slippery. Hearing her shuffling towards him George raised his head and put out his hand as if to aid her. She made a valiant effort to smile at him, but succeeded only in moving her lips to the slightest degree. Her eyes, black-rimmed with fatigue, were lightless and staring.

Tears sprang to George's eyes as he remembered how hard they had fought for their lives, battering at the door with the wooden bier, breaking the windows, tearing their clothes into ribbons in order to make a rope, so that one of them might climb up to those accursed windows, set so high, and fall through. To break every bone in one's body was nothing compared to this long, slow nightmare. But there had been nothing to which the rope could be attached, no hook or projection in that shiny mosaic-work which lined every wall, and which had been discreetly admired by all the Sussex gentry who had been invited to attend Darker interments. They were trapped in a smooth, brightly-coloured tomb. The beautful mosaic of Christ in Majesty, worked on the ceiling, seemed to mock them with large, mournful eyes.

Sarah was making feeble flapping motions with her hands in an effort to attract her brother's attention. She whispered, "Do you carry your derringer in your pocket?"

"Yes."

"Is it loaded?"

"Yes."

"Both chambers?"

"Yes."

She gave a defeated little sigh. "Then that must be the way of it." He had already thought of that way out, but had not liked to suggest it to her. Apparently he had under-estimated the strength of her spirit. His throat made a harsh, rattling sound, like a file on metal, as he tried to clear it. "Not yet."

She looked frightened. "We must not wait until you have not the strength . . . to pull . . . the trigger." Talking had exhausted her. She now laboured to draw breath between each word or two.

"At least another two days," he assured her. "I can still walk unaided."

"Yes, you are in better case than I."

His eyes went again to the marks on the wall. "Perhaps Mama will come soon." Slowly, she keeled over sideways, and with her cheek pressed to the tiles said in a drowsy murmur, "We are being punished for our sins."

George fingered the coarse growth of stubble which fretted his chin. "If I emerge from this state of purgatory alive I shall freely confess to father that I am not Francis. Lucy can divorce me, and I shall join the army. It may be that I can make up for what I did by serving my country."

"I shall . . . stay with Thomas . . . and Mr Cobbett."

He asked, "What shall we do with the money and the jewellery?"

Again he thought she had fallen asleep, because she was so long in responding, but at last she managed, "Put . . . the sack . . . down in the vault . . . now, while you . . . still have the strength."

The trap-door leading to the vault gaped open, just as he had left it when he had struggled up the slime-drenched steps with the bier to make his fruitless assault upon the door. With an effort he scrambled to his feet, and staggering slightly, like a man in his cups, went over to where the sack containing the proceeds of their nine robberies lay beneath one of the benches in the arcade. With his foot he pushed it, inch by inch, towards the opening in the floor. It tipped over and disappeared down the steps with a muffled jingling sound. If he and Sarah were to die the sack would not be discovered until their bodies, according to custom, were placed in the vault, one year after death. On the other hand, if they managed to survive this ordeal, five or six years might pass before it came to light, since Grandpapa Darker showed no signs at present of failing health.

George averted his eyes from the pile of excreta in the corner and made his way back to his sister, who, on hands and knees, was now dragging herself towards the altar. She reached it, and her hands came up to grasp the edge of the table. The altar-cloth came away in her hands and she fell back with a low, whimpering moan.

Claudine Darker, dressed for the outdoors in pelisse and bonnet, made a little tut of annoyance as she walked past her daughter-in-law's bedroom. Sounds of weeping were clearly audible. Claudine had no patience left for Lucy. The girl had driven her son away by her incessant nagging, and by her failure to produce a child. Having borne three children in one go Claudine was at a loss to understand how any woman was unable to manage at least one.

When Francis had disappeared she had done her best to comfort Lucy, assuring the girl that her husband would return in a day or so, but the constant moanings and repinings were beginning to get on her nerves, and she now shunned any contact with her daughter-in-law, taking her meals in her room until the storm should be past.

Having recovered from the initial shock of hearing that her son and daughter had run away Claudine was of the opinion that Francis and Sarah would come home in less than a fortnight. They had, she was sure, gone to London for a little pleasure and recreation. As far as Francis was concerned the first was to be found with a whore, and the second in gaming clubs and coffee-houses. Sarah would probably spend her time gazing into the windows of the shops in Oxford Street, and perhaps marvelling at the beautiful new buildings which were being erected by John Nash between the Prince Regent's London residence of Carlton House and the City Park.

Claudine descended the stairs soft-footed, anxious only that Lucy should not hear her and come begging for sympathy. As she rounded the turn of the stair she caught sight of a basket of blooms which had been placed in the hall in readiness for her to take down to the mausoleum. It was not her day for changing the flowers, and although James had forbidden her to leave the house, because Dr Pettit had not yet given his permission for her to sample the air after her bout of influenza, Claudine had decided to take matters into her own hands, and had given orders for the flowers to be cut. She thought that James would not scold her too much for disobeying him. A short walk would greatly refresh her after having been shut up in the house for a week.

Claudine was about to pick up the basket containing the flowers when she remembered that she required the key to enter the mausoleum. It was strange how one could forget simple things like that after so short a break from normal routine. She walked through the hall, past the servants' staircase, and into the wide passage leading to the kitchens. Hunting prints lined the walls of this small slip-room which was used by family and servants alike. One such print, taking pride of place among the others, depicted a stallion called "Frinton" which had won the Gold Plate at Newmarket in the year 1780.

Claudine removed the mausoleum key from its hook, at the same time smiling a greeting at Mrs Barrett, the sempstress, who had just entered the house by the back entrance and was now walking round to the front of the house. Claudine's greeting was cheerful, "Good-morning, Mrs Barrett. Please to go upstairs and begin upon the blue taffeta. I shall be back for a fitting in about an hour."

Mrs Barrett smiled broadly. "Is the blue taffeta for the Brighton races, ma'am? If so, I've to make haste."

Claudine nodded. "I am sure that you will do very well, Mrs Barrett. You always manage to have things ready on time."

Mrs Barrett curtseyed and passed on. She enjoyed working in the Darker household more than anywhere else in the county. Mrs Darker was such an appreciative lady, praising everything that was made for her, and didn't she look something in the finished articles, not like that skinny creature Mrs Lucy. Things hung on that one like a sack, unless they were padded and flounced and puffed every which way. Mrs Barrett's pride and joy in her customer might have been somewhat dimmed had she known that Mrs Darker, when she really wanted to "shine" in company, employed a Brighton dressmaker to stitch more splendid gowns for her. With exquisite tact Claudine kept these special gowns well out of sight.

Claudine followed Mrs Barrett back into the hall—at a discreet distance, of course, because one never walked alongside servants—and rang the footmen's bell. Then she picked up the basket and waited. Albert, the under-footman, aged fifteen, was in the hall in three seconds and moved swiftly to open the front door, bowing Claudine out with a "G'morning, ma'am," and an impish smile. Claudine patted his curly head and informed him, "You will never make a *head* footman, Albert, unless you learn to go about with a very solemn countenance."

"No, ma'am," he agreed demurely. She gave his cheek a little pat. "For my part, I prefer you just as you are, Albert, but that shall remain a secret between us." Albert blushed furiously and wished that he could do something really brave for Mrs Darker to show her how much he liked her.

The first thing that Claudine noticed as she approached the mausoleum was a large carrion crow perched on the roof. Even as she stopped to stare the bird flapped its wings and flew off, but not very far. It came to rest on a nearby oak tree, clumsily folding its huge black wings, thrusting forward its head in a curious questing movement and noisily cawing its dislike of intruders. Claudine could not take her eyes off it. Was it a bird of ill-omen? It looked so threatening, hanging there, as if it were about to pounce on its prey.

She continued to watch the bird and walked forward to

open the wrought-iron gate. As she stepped on to the brick path a shiver ran down her spine and she squared her shoulders, commanding herself to dismiss morbid thoughts from her mind. She was associating the crow with the mausoleum. Together they spelled the word death. The crow had probably set up its calling-post in the oak tree quite by chance. There was nothing more sinister in it than that.

But what was this? Claudine stumbled upon an object which lay in her path, and looking down was astonished to see the gold chalice which normally had its resting-place on the altar in the mausoleum. Wonderingly, she put down her basket and bent to retrieve the chalice, pausing only to look upwards for a brief, frightened glance at the stained-glass windows, four of which, she was alarmed to discover, were broken. Her heart started to race, and her first thought was that thieves had been at work. They would be gone by now, she reasoned resolutely, so there could be no danger if she ventured inside the building. With the chalice in her hand, therefore, and taking the key from the pocket of her pelisse, she advanced towards the door. The key turned like silk in the lock. Claudine pushed the door inwards, stepped inside, and with a startled exclamation recoiled at the smell which assailed her nostrils. A split-second later her eyes were registering a little *tableau* positioned before the altar. Her mouth opened in a scream.

James Darker finished his morning inspection of the stable-block, and after instructing the Head Groom to have his stallion saddled and brought round to the front of the house at precisely eleven o'clock, he returned to the house, replacing in his breeches pocket a white handkerchief which he had used to test the cleanliness of the horses' coats. Many a stable-lad had walked into the flat of the master's hand when the handkerchief came away even slightly soiled. As James emerged from the stable-court, passing under the little bell-tower and out on to the driveway, he caught sight of a figure running across the park from the direction of the mausoleum.

It was a moment or two before he recognised Claudine, for his unconscious mind had relegated her to the safety of the house. His first reaction was one of annoyance that she had disobeyed the instructions of Dr. Pettit. Then his ear picked up a sort of high-pitched moaning sound which his brain directly connected with the flying figure, and in a trice he was running to meet his wife. He knew, as his feet pounded the turf what she had discovered. As he drew nearer he could see a single yellow chrysanthemum clinging to her pink furred pelisse. Her bonnet hung by its ribbons at the back of her head, and her dark hair, carefully dressed that morning, had escaped from its silver pins. She threw herself into his arms, babbling nonsense, sobbing out disconnected words which would have made no sense to him had he not already guessed the nature of the shock she had but a moment before received. He admitted to a fleeting instant of fear as he wondered if he had over-estimated his children's powers of endurance.

Gathering Claudine up in his arms he ran with her towards the house. "Sarah . . . Francis . . . are they dead? Oh, God, how horrible . . . Christ help my dear children . . . in their own filth and blood . . . Sarah had blood on her arm. . . ." Startled footmen followed the master's rapid progress up the stairs and scurried away as James bawled over his shoulder, "Send for Dr. Pettit . . . at once!"

Mrs Barrett looked up in amazement as James entered his wife's bedroom and crossing to the bed deposited Claudine's limp figure on to the quilted coverlet. "Oh, sir!" The sempstress laid aside her work and hurried to the bedside. "Is Mrs Darker taken ill again?"

"I am afraid so," James returned gravely. "I think it was extremely ill-advised of her to take the air before she was quite recovered."

"But she looked so well this morning," Mrs Barrett said with a puzzled frown. "Quite blooming, in fact, and in excellent spirits."

James too was frowning. "Her looks, I fear, were deceptive, Mrs Barrett. Will you please to leave us alone? The physician will be here on the instant." His tone was pleasantly authoritative and Mrs Barrett was quite used to being summarily dismissed. Without another word she left the room. As she closed the door behind her she heard Claudine say, "Blood . . . my children." Mrs Barrett clucked her tongue sympathetically and told herself that it was none of her business. The poor lady was delirious anyway, and did not know what she was saying.

James moved swiftly when the sempstress had gone. Claudine kept a medicine chest in her bedroom, a small oaken cupboard in fact, free standing, which opened to reveal a series of little drawers fitted with knobs of chased brass. James opened the drawer marked "Laudanum—liquid," situated above that marked "Opium—pills" and took from it a blue ribbed bottle. A little tray beneath the drawer provided a silver spoon. Armed with these two items he returned to his wife's side.

It occurred to James that something might be seriously wrong with Claudine. She was still noisily delirious. Was it wise to administer laudanum while a person was in that state? It was imperative, however, to keep her quiet until he could deal with the problem in the mausoleum. It seemed that the long wait must be terminated quickly in that quarter. Claudine had spoken of blood. Things had obviously deteriorated to a greater degree than he had anticipated or intended when he had decided that seven days would be the limit of his children's ability to survive without food and water. He reflected wryly that it was just like Claudine to run away without first ascertaining just how serious the situation was, or to offer help to the young people, about whom she seemed so much concerned that she had fallen into a stupor.

Carefully, James measured out four drops of laudanum and forced the spoon between his wife's teeth. She was fairly passive now, and he saw her throat muscles contract as she swallowed the draught. It would be enough to keep her calm until the physician had come and gone, and it would give him a breathing space to do what had to be done in the mausoleum.

James made all haste round to the stable-block and harnessed the phaeton with his own hands, much to the amazement of the stable-lads, who were impatiently brushed aside when they offered their assistance. Jack Gander came down from his room in the loft to observe these operations, and was politely requested to fill a half-gallon milk churn to the brim with water and to place the aforesaid container in the back of the phaeton along with a dipper.

Of all James's servants Jack Gander was the most trustworthy, a man to whom one could confide a secret and know that it would never be revealed, not even to his nearest and dearest. Long in the service of the Darker family, having taken over from his uncle in the year 1779, Jack knew no other way of life, and remained secure in the knowledge that he would stay at Frinton Park until the day he died.

"I am taking the phaeton upon a most particular errand, Jack," James told him in a low voice, "an errand, the nature of which I shall later make known to the members of my household. I shall not, I think, be gone above one half-hour, and when you hear me return I shall be greatly obliged if you will make sure that your boys are out of the way. The phaeton and "Little Beauty" shall be returned to their customary places, and as far as you are concerned, there is an end to the matter."

Jack Gander made a final adjustment to the mare's harness, just to prove that the master was poaching on his sole preserves, and employing the rough tact of his kind inquired abruptly, "Shall you be needin' 'Tarquin' to go into Lewes today, sir? It be your day for the bank if I'm not mistaken?"

The question was entirely superfluous, posed only to bridge a difficult gap in this exchange between master and servant, and James immediately recognised it as such. He wished that those who inhabited his own social sphere could be as discreet as Jack. Less than an hour ago he had given orders for his stallion to be saddled and ready by eleven o'clock. He now repeated them as if they had never been issued. "Yes, Jack, you are right. I shall be requiring 'Tarquin'. Have him saddled and round at the front door by eleven o'clock, if you please, and tell that young rascal William that the next time he saddles 'Lady Violet' for my wife he should remember that Mrs Darker's legs have the proportions of those of a normal female personage. They are not approaching four feet in length. Last time he brought out 'Lady Violet' her stirrups were practically trailing the ground."

"I'll beat the livin' daylights out of 'un, sir, if 'e do do it again," promised Jack grimly. "There now, sir, she'm quite ready."

Arrived at the mausoleum James was quick to notice the broken windows, and his lips tightened in an exclamation of annoyance. They would cost him a pretty penny to replace. As he approached the door of the building a gleam of silver caught his eye, which, upon investigation, proved to be a candlestick. He left it where is was, thinking that Francis—no, George . . . he must get used to that—had exerted the strength of desperation. Those windows were high.

Once inside the mausoleum the smell almost drove him back, but there was no time for hesitation. His erring children were in sad case. Claudine had warned him that one of them had some sort of wound and, sure enough, there was blood all over Sarah's left arm. A knife? No, the explanation lay in the discarded derringer which lay beside the clumsily sprawled form of his son. The fool had tried to shoot his sister with a snap-hance pocket pistol, that lady's toy.

Armed with the milk-churn James moved towards the almost motionless figures and deposited his burden on the floor. Sarah, dimly sensing his approach, lifted her head and whispered, "Mama . . . she screamed . . . she went away. Why did she go away? I could not move nor cry out. . . ."

Supporting his daughter's head upon one arm and manipulating the dipper with the other James offered her a drink. She sucked in the water noisily, and he had to restrain her from drinking too much. He felt no spark of tenderness for the pale, thin creature she had become, only a deep, abiding anger that she had put the Darker good name in jeopardy . . . for the second time. His drastic action was, he felt, fully justified. He had reduced both his children to a proper humility. In future they would know how to behave. That he had brought them very close to death did not unduly disturb him. Had their activities been uncovered, as they surely must have been in due time, they would both have faced the prospect of transportation to the convict colony in Australia. James was still happily ignorant of the fact that his son had committed murder, or the hangman's rope would have figured in his imaginings.

He pulled Sarah to her feet and supporting her with his arm about her waist walked with her to the phaeton. Picking her up in his arms he placed her on the back seat with the harsh injunction to "Show a little backbone and sit up, if you please, Sarah."

She did her best, her shoulders rounded with fatigue, her head drooping, the blood brown and congealed on her arm where the ball from the derringer had grazed her. When James went back inside the building he found George sitting up and imbibing the water with a series of spluttering gulps. When he saw his father the young man rose unsteadily to his feet and essaying a few lurching steps forward, endeavoured to cling to James's neck, at the same time gasping out some sort of confession. Yes, thought James complacently as he listened to the contrite words, he had reduced them to a very proper humility.

James found it more difficult to support the weight of his son, and staggered a little as George leaned heavily upon him. A hand under the other's rump assisted him into the phaeton, where he slumped beside his sister, the pair of them looking as though they had just been dragged from a debtor's prison. James decided that the cleansing of the mausoleum would have to be deferred until the evening. The task, though distasteful, must be carried out by the master himself.

After locking the door behind him James drove the phaeton at a smart pace back to the stable-block. Immediately upon entering the house, having instructed Sarah and George to wait on the steps for exactly five minutes before coming in, he summoned the servants to assemble in the front hall, ready with a dramatic tale to the effect that his children had been returning home from an unauthorised excursion to London, like Biblical prodigals, when they had been set upon by ruffians, tied up and left to die. After lying bound and gagged for three days upon Ditchlcy Common they had succeeded in breaking loose at last and had dragged themselves home, collapsing at the very gates of Frinton Park, where their father had chanced to come upon them as he was just about to embark upon an inspection of broken fence palings. He had run back to the stables for the phaeton, and Sarah and Francis were now brought safely home. They must be put to bed at once, but there was no necessity for the physician to be troubled because what they really required was rest and sustenance. They would be as right as rain in a day or two.

Mrs Barrett, who had come into the hall with the rest, more from curiosity than because she was required to do so, offered it as her opinion that if Dr Pettit had already been summoned to attend upon Mrs Darker he might just as well cast his professional eye over young Mr Darker and Mrs Cobbett. Heavens above, but didn't they look seedy! This as the torn, dishevelled figures of Sarah and George made their belated appearance in the hall. James had deliberately allowed them to support each other into the house in order to give the impression that medical assistance was not required.

The pair were somewhat sharply bidden to go upstairs. They obeyed their father, slowly and unsteadily, followed by the aghast stares of the servants, who thought that the master was being over-zealous in his desire to punish them for what was, after all, "only a bit of a lark."

James impaled Mrs Barrett with a look which would have quelled a woman of lesser spirit. "They will do well enough after they have rested and partaken of food, Mrs Barrett. I shall not put Dr. Pettit to the trouble of examining them." James had a very good reason for this. He did not want George and Sarah to embark upon a verbal exchange with anyone until he had had a chance to speak his own mind, and to lay down a set of rules for their future conduct. No doubt they believed that they had been locked into the mausoleum by accident. He would quickly disillusion them on that score. They should be made well aware that they had been punished for their crimes, and that he was now privy to another even more disgraceful secret which they had inadvertently revealed as they plotted their devilry.

"But the blood on Mrs Cobbett's arm," bleated Mrs Barrett, oblivious of the steely gleam in the master's eye. "The poor young lady looks as though she has been badly hurt." As if to give emphasis to these words Sarah, to everyone's horror, had collapsed on the upper landing and was being hauled unceremoniously to her feet by George, who shot a reproachful look at his father standing in the hall below.

James did not budge an inch from his unbending attitude, and cut Mrs Barrett off short when she made as if to go upstairs to Sarah's assistance. "Mrs Barrett!" he thundered, "if you should presume to interfere with the running of my household you will very soon find yourself out of it . . . for good!"

At this Mrs Barrett, her cheeks flaming with colour, backed away from the stairs. Mrs Claudine Darker was a very good customer. Not only that, if one were to give offence in the house of a "county" family the word would soon get around, and she would be banned from working in other big houses. Mrs Barrett, who was not inclined to quarrel with her bread and butter, beat a hasty retreat.

Dr. Pettit looked knowledgeable and extremely solemn. It was regrettable that Mrs Darker had taken it upon herself to disobey his explicit instructions. Her foolishness—hastily he begged James's pardon—her *high spirits* could have serious consequences upon her general health. He feared very much that she had had a brain-storm.

After tut-tutting at some length over Claudine's condition the good doctor prescribed nourishing soups and the four-hourly administration of two drops of laudanum until the patient began to show signs of recovery. He would have staked his reputation upon Mrs Darker having received some kind of shock. No? Most extraordinary. Dr. Pettit went on his way, shaking his head in disbelief.

As dusk was creeping over the park James, equipped with mops and a bucket, trudged across to the mausoleum, his thoughts occupied by the recent interview he had had with his white-faced children. They had been shocked and dismayed to learn that it had been their own dear Papa who had kept them prisoner for almost a week. They had professed themselves as entirely repentant, and had promised to do better in the future, abiding by the unwritten but rigid code laid down for the high-spirited younger members of a large and wealthy family. The change of identities between Francis and George must remain a secret for the time being, but it was to be devoutly hoped, when Francis returned from the wars, that the mess could be sorted out, although James confessed himself presently quite at a loss to know how this might be done. Neither Claudine nor Lucy must be told, he had insisted firmly.

James entered the mausoleum and did what had to be done. The sack of paper money and jewels was just visible on the bottom step of the flight leading down to the vault. With a grimace James decided to leave it where it was. He closed the trap-door. The sack might stay there until he came to some conclusion as to what should be done with its contents.

From a nearby well, dedicated to St. Winifred, which was fed from a tributary of the River Adur, James drew water and thoroughly cleansed the floor of the mausoleum. The blood-stained altar-cloth he removed. Next, the gold and silver altar furnishings were retrieved from the garden and replaced, including the chalice which Claudine had dropped again in her shock and fright. The broken windows told their own story and remained the only clearly visible evidence of what had happened. Later they could be repaired, doubtless at an exorbitant cost to himself. The scratch marks on the wall, the purpose of which he immediately divined, there being six of them, must be painted out until a skilled mosaic-worker could be found to replace the defaced pieces.

James took a last look round, picked up his mops and bucket, and locking the mausoleum door behind him tramped back to the house.

The Eavesdropper

Within three days Sarah and George were fully recovered from their ordeal and Sarah made preparations to return to her husband. She had tried very hard to delay her departure from Frinton Park, on the pretext that her mother was not yet restored to health, but James was insistent that her place was beside Mr Cobbett and little Thomas. She did not think it worth the effort to argue with her father, knowing that he now held her future firmly in the palm of his hand, and might destroy her at any time he pleased if she failed to obey him. Unlike George, Sarah's repentance was short-lived. Now that the threat of immediate death had receded, she had conveniently forgotten her desire to reform and thought herself very hard done-by.

Brother and sister were taking chocolate in the Morning Room, George merely passing the time until his father should declare himself ready to go into Lewes, where the two were to attend an auction of farm implements, Sarah putting off for as long as possible the evil hour when she must return to the school-master's cottage. She was certain of no very good reception there. Mr Cobbett had already been twice to Frinton Park to lecture her on her obligations as a wife and mother, and had uttered dark threats about the penalties for future misbehaviour.

Sarah sipped her chocolate, made a face and added to it another spoonful of brown Barbados sugar. "I still find it hard to believe that Papa could have done such a truly dreadful thing," she remarked in aggrieved tones. "He might well have condemned us to death."

George shrugged. "What he overheard in the mausoleum made him very angry indeed. It is my opinion that he was more incensed by my having changed places with Francis than he was at discovering we were thieves."

"Did you tell him about that Pinkerton girl?" she probed anxiously.

"Yes. He was less disturbed than I had imagined he would be. She was a woman of little consequence."

"Did you *have* to kill her?"

George bit his lip. He was not proud of that particular incident. "She was a whore who knew rather too much for her own good, and there was a witness."

"It was pique though all the same, was it not?" Sarah said with a knowing smile. "You were out of temper because she had had the foresight to place her money in the bank."

The truth pained him, and he had no desire to look it in the face. His voice had a self-righteous ring as he replied, "I only wanted what was mine. She took me for three-and-a-half thousand pounds. As I pointed out to her at the time I regarded the money as a loan."

Sarah giggled. "It was not yours to lend, dear George. It was my dowry, the loss of which Mr Cobbett still mourns."

"Such an amount would have been wasted in the hands of Cobbett. A man like that does not know how to make his money work for him."

Sarah, who now disliked her husband so much that she could hardly bear to hear his name mentioned, was off on another tack. "Do you really believe that Papa would carry out his threat to expose us if we tried to return to our wicked ways?"

"Do not doubt it for an instant," George advised her.

"Mama is to be kept in ignorance of the whole thing. She believes that we have been to see the sights of London." Sarah looked worried. "I wish I knew what Papa means to do when Francis comes home."

George toyed with the spoon in his saucer, tapping it against the side of his cup. "It is his wish that we resume our rightful places."

His sister frowned and argued, "But that will not serve at all. Francis is bound to look quite different now. His skin will be brown from long exposure to the sun, and he will be thinner, much thinner. I remember when Reggie Lambton came back from the Portuguese expedition in 1811 we scarcely recognised him, and he looked as though he had aged a million years."

"Nevertheless," George countered, "Papa is determined that we shall be given back our original identities. He says it is unthinkable that we should remained as we are for the rest of our lives. He is even prepared to engage a lawyer to sort out the muddle."

"And Mrs Lucy is supposed to take another man to her bed and not know the difference? Is she to be told nothing? Papa should bear in mind that when Lucy married you, accepting you as Francis, she did not know either of you at all well. Now that you and Lucy have lived together as man and wife I cannot imagine that she could be duped a second time."

George sighed dispiritedly. "My head aches with it all. For my part, I shall bide my time and see what happens. I counsel you to do the same."

She pouted. "I do not know how I shall endure the company of Mr Cobbett."

"You may take it from me that it is surprising what one can do when one tries," returned George unsympathetically.

She was close to tears. "The thought of all that money going to waste makes my heart bleed. Papa says he will give the money to charitable causes, but that the jewels are to remain hidden unless he can find a means of returning them to their rightful owners without arousing suspicion."

She gave a shaky little laugh. "Can you imagine Mrs Lambton's face if she were to discover that her rather shoddy necklace is now reposing in some locked cupboard or drawer in Frinton Park, proceeds of a robbery cleverly executed by Mr George Darker and his sister Sarah?"

George was beginning to grow tired of Sarah's continual harping upon a subject which he now found distasteful. Although before Sarah he put up a show of believing that he had done nothing which someone else, placed in exactly similar circumstances would not have done, he was thoroughly ashamed of his fall from grace, which had begun to take on something of the quality of a nightmare. Wakeful in the night, he would frequently ask himself questions to which he could find no satisfactory answers. Had he really murdered a young woman simply because she had roused him to anger? Had he left a stunned man to burn to death? Had he degenerated into a common thief, who desired no other way of life? Worse than all these things in his own estimation, had he forfeited his father's regard for ever? As is so often the case with repentant criminals George looked about him for someone or something on which to lay the blame for his own unutterable folly. Inevitably his choice fell upon Sarah, who, by her suggestion that her two brothers change places, had been the instigator of the whole series of disasters which had descended upon the family. Sarah was the direct cause of all his present troubles, the interloper between twin brothers, the destroyer of their happiness. He said aloud, "You had better forget all that. Put it behind you and begin life anew. It is time you settled down anyway."

Her eyebrows lifted in sardonic amusement. "Your virtue astounds me. So we are no longer in accord, you and I?"

"Not if you persist in raking over the ashes of the past."

She drank in these words with the last of her chocolate and announced casually, "I have it in mind to keep to our original plan and go to London . . . when all the fuss has died down that is."

"And live on your wits I suppose?"

She bit her lip savagely. "Before I go I mean to repossess myself of what is mine! Having gone to a deal of trouble to get it I am not willing to give up my money without a fight."

Her words angered him. "Then you are a bigger fool than I took you for. Pray tell me how you shall contrive to persuade Mr Wilkins of the Lewes bank to hand over seven thousand pounds? He will. . . ."

A shout of laughter interrupted his argument. "It is you, George, who are the fool. Do you really think it likely that Papa has deposited *stolen* bills and jewellery in the bank? Would not Mr Wilkins express some surprise to be asked to guard a quantity of jewellery, when he knows that Mama loves to deck herself out with every piece she possesses, and has never been persuaded to give him her more expensive items for safe keeping? And might he not recognise some of the pieces? He loves to tread a measure, and there is not a rout or a ball in the county which does not see him present with his trail of marriageable daughters. He must have seen that wretched Lambton necklace a hundred times. No, George. Our money and jewels are hidden somewhere in this house. You may depend upon it."

Her words made him pensive, and he sat staring at his cup of cooling chocolate as though he expected to gain inspiration from the rich, dark liquid.

"I believe that Papa has hidden the money and jewels in some very secret place which will take a deal of ferreting out."

The remark, dropped into the lengthening silence, repeated itself over and over again in George's head, and a brief inward struggle took place, during which he weighed the odds for and against resuming his criminal way of life. The outcome, however, was never in doubt, for George Darker had looked into the mouth of hell and liked not what he had seen. He levelled a long, intimidating stare at his sister. "If you endeavour to steal the money again from Papa you may not count upon me for support."

"Ah, so you are determined upon being a good little Darker from now on," she sneered.

"You may safely depend upon it."

"If I am caught I shall say that you helped me," she threatened.

His face darkened and his pale eyes bulged with fury. "Then you would do well to remember that I killed the last female who tried to hold me up to ransom!"

She fell silent, not really believing that he meant what he said, but realising at the same time that there was no help coming from that quarter.

The door of the Morning Room opened and Claudine walked into the charged atmosphere to ask her daughter if she meant to walk down to the village, or would she like to borrow the gig? Sarah answered sullenly that she would prefer to walk, and unfairly despised her mother for her refusal to admit that anything at all untoward had occurred. She must guess *something*. Claudine, despite her scatter-brained habits, was no fool. Sarah wondered what her mother would think if the whole truth were to be revealed to her. She decided that Claudine would probably go quite mad.

Three members of the Darker family left the Morning Room. A fourth emerged rather dazedly from behind the curtained window-seat and sat down in a chair to think.

AUGUST, 1815

Lucy puts a finger in the pie. . . .

For a long time Lucy was not quite sure what to do with her new-found knowledge. Her bemused mind had taken a day or two to assimilate its significance. She at length came to the conclusion that she was not inclined to expose her husband and sister-in-law in the matter of their criminal activities, since some of the stigma attaching to them must surely cling to her. This left that other, infinitely more shocking revelation to be considered, to wit, that the man she had married was not the man to whom she had been betrothed, and to whom she had given her heart. She had been the victim of a most cruel and heartless deception. Worse, she had been made to look a fool, and her openly expressed attachment to Francis—the ramblings of an idiot she now knew, for only an idiot could be tricked into accepting a substitution for the adored one—must surely have caused George a certain amount of under-the-sleeve amusement.

The more she thought about it the worse it seemed in terms of sheer mean-spirited chicanery. Francis could hardly have offered her a more crushing insult than to have carelessly palmed her off on to his brother. As for George, he was to be utterly despised for his part in the sordid affair. The fact that George had once truly loved her Lucy refused even to take into account, or that her sharp tongue had been largely responsible for the rift which, like a yawning chasm, had now opened up between them. Of one thing Lucy was quite certain. Both Francis and George deserved to be punished for what they had done to her.

Mrs Lucy Darker, with her love of all things domestic, with her yearning to become the sole mistress of a large country mansion, did not seem cut out for the role of avenging angel, but it is marvellous what a woman scorned is capable of doing when she sets her mind to it.

It was not until after Francis—still masquerading as George and noticeably avoiding her eye—had returned from the war, and had been once more drawn into the bosom of his family, that Lucy had put her preconceived plan into action. She had been made aware by her eavesdropping that James Darker would very much like to have seen his sons resume their true identities, and was sad in the knowledge that this might never be possible, for Francis, as Sarah had so accurately predicted, had returned from Europe a completely changed man. He was much thinner now than his brother, and his features had taken on the hard, leathery look of a man much exposed to the elements. His fair hair had been bleached almost white by the sun, and there was a deep scar running from his right ear to the corner of his mouth, reminder of a sabre-cut received in the heat of battle, hardly noticed at the time and not in the least worth mentioning in his letters home. It showed up as a livid purple line against his brown skin and had caused Claudine to draw in her breath in dismay when she first caught sight of it.

Francis's manner was different too. He was strangely economic of speech, and addressed both family and servants in sharp, clipped sentences, barking out words as though he were still issuing orders to a ghostly company of men, some of whom had long since dispersed to various dwellings all over England, others of whom lay beneath the soil of the field of Waterloo, their bodies providing sustenance for a host of fine harvests to come. No, thought Lucy, there could be no possibility of putting to rights now what had been put wrong all those months ago.

Lucy had laid her plans well. Nine months ago, when she had sat curled up, still as a mouse, in the Morning

Room, listening to Sarah spitting defiance and declaring her intention of retrieving "what is mine," she had been certain of only one thing. She, who had the advantage of living permanently in Frinton Park, would discover the whereabouts of that cache of money and jewels before either George—who, judging by his attitude did not represent much of a threat anyway—or Sarah could lay their hands upon it. Then, armed with her secret knowledge, she might be able to devise a plan whereby she could get her own back on her arrogant Darker cousins.

Lucy had set about her search that very day, combing the house, going from room to room and poking her nose into every nook and cranny which offered itself as a possible hiding-place for illicit goods. After a month of this she had had to admit to herself that she was beaten. Not an inch of Frinton Park but had come under her scrutiny, not a clue as to the whereabouts of what she so ardently sought manifested itself. It was some consolation to her to know that Sarah, on the few occasions when she came to the house, was similarly thwarted. Lucy watched her sister-in-law like the proverbial cat, never letting the other out of her sight without first ascertaining that she was gone about some business which would keep her occupied for an hour or two. Sometimes it made Lucy smile to watch Sarah steal away in the direction of the library, or to the upper regions of the house, and she would laugh inside herself when Sarah returned with a small frown creasing her brow and a look of puzzlement mixed with irritation in her eyes.

The thought that the money and jewellery might be hidden in the mausoleum came to Lucy like a flash of lightning one day in the summer of 1815 when she had been helping Claudine to pick flowers for the altar. Plucking up courage she had gone with her mother-in-law to help arrange the flowers, receiving a nod of approval and a remark to the effect that she was at last showing a little commonsense, for there was nothing at all to be feared from the dead. "Only the living, my dear Lucy, have the power to hurt you," Claudine had said, with so much irony in her tone that Lucy had wondered just what this cryptic statement might mean.

A quick glance round the mausoleum had informed Lucy that there was no possible place where anything might be hidden. Contriving to peep behind the altar when Claudine was not looking her way she had been confronted with a blank curtained space, and the vestment box, with its lid thrown back, was too glaringly obvious to be worth further inspection.

Lucy had been about to resign herself to the fact that she had drawn yet another blank when her foot had encountered an unfamiliar surface. She looked down and saw the trap-door, and her heart gave a great lurch. She would never be able to go down there! At the same time as she thought this it also occurred to Lucy that if she could get up enough stomach to go down into the vault she would certainly have shown herself to be the equal, if not the superior of Sarah in boldness.

It had rather irked Lucy to discover that her sister-in-law had engaged in such daring escapades as had come to light in the Morning Room. Though operating outside the law Sarah's activities had somehow seemed to Lucy to smack of romance and adventure, the sort one read about in novels borrowed from Mr Thomas's circulating library in Brighton. Before becoming obsessed with Miss Austen, whose name was now known to the world at large, Lucy, like Sarah, had had a penchant for Maria Edgeworth, and had thrilled to the exploits of frightened heroines as they picked their dangerous way through one hundred and fifty thousand words.

If only she could bring herself to venture down into that black hole, with its harvest of coffins and dusty, dried-out wreaths. A couple of glasses of Mr Darker's very fine claret perhaps, taken a few minutes beforehand to boost one's courage? There would be nothing to *see* down there she had told herself firmly, nothing terrifying that is. Only a few coffins set upon biers. "The dead cannot harm you, Lucy, only the living. . . ." Lucy repeated Claudine's words over and over again to herself like a good-luck incantation. By the time she had returned to the house her mind had been made up.

On an afternoon in early July, fortified by two glasses of claret, and with the key to the mausoleum in the pocket of her pelisse, Lucy stole down to the family resting-place and without giving herself time to think, slipped inside and closed the door behind her. The afternoon sun sent a shaft of light slanting through one of the newly replaced stained-glass windows, sprinkling the altar with red, blue, green and purple spots of colour, creating a pleasant, homely atmosphere which dispelled some of Lucy's fear.

At first the trap-door had resisted her efforts to raise it, but the strength of determination came to Lucy's aid and she at last managed to fling it back. The steps down were steep and difficult to negotiate. Lucy had not essayed more than two when she remembered that she would need a light if she was to see anything at all in that sinister, yawning blackness. She would have to run back to the house for candle and tinder-box. She was about to retreat when a patch of deeper blackness attracted her sharp young eyes. There was something at the foot of the steps. Another cautious step down and she was peering into the gloom below. It looked like a sack down there. Lucy took a deep breath, ran down the remaining steps, careless of the fact that they were a thought slippery, and grabbed hold of the formless bundle. It was not too heavy. Thankfully she turned about and re-mounted the steps, dragging her burden after her. Panting as if she had run a mile she slammed down the trap-door and sank to the floor before her knees finally gave way.

A rapid inspection of the contents of the sack revealed to Lucy's astonished gaze her grandmother's pearl necklace, Mrs Lambton's diamond throat collar, and Lady Oliver's ruby necklace . . . and to whom did that sapphire brooch belong? Lucy knew that she had seen it somewhere before. Heavens, it belonged to Mama! So that unscrupulous pair had actually stolen from their own mother!

Lucy bided her time—for no better reason than that she wanted to savour her triumph in secret for a week or two—until a hot day in August when the whole family were to go to Brighton to attend one of the Regent's garden parties. As the carriage bowled away down the drive of Frinton Park, Lucy, tucked into a corner seat, permitted herself a small, anticipatory smile. She felt entirely satisfied that she had chosen a good day to astonish the family with her cleverness.

. . . and states her terms

That evening Claudine was positively sprightly at the supper-table, for the Prince Regent, rotund and smiling graciously, had deigned to speak to her, and had complimented her on her hat, which he had described as having "the odour of Paris, ma'am." After a beautifully executed curtsey Claudine had explained with pride that her son, who had fought at Waterloo, had brought it back with him from abroad, and that it had indeed been purchased in Paris. "Ah, the brave fellow," the Regent had answered, panting a little at the exertion of walking round the garden in his steel corset. "Was he wounded, ma'am?" Claudine had admitted, again with pride, that her son had received a slight facial wound, indicating with a graceful gesture of her hand Francis's blemished and embarrassed face.

The Regent had leaned forward to inspect this mark, received for the honour of England, and had nodded his head several times in approval. "Brave fellow," he repeated, adding suprisingly, "I intend to visit the field of Waterloo myself as soon as it can be arranged. I am anxious to see the tree under which Lord Uxbridge's leg is buried."

"What *presence* he has," enthused Claudine as she plied her knife and fork.

"A very large presence," chuckled James.

Claudine ignored this implied criticism of her new idol. She smiled at Lucy. "It was fortunate, was it not, that we were privileged to witness such an astonishingly *grand* spectacle, my dear Lucy? It is to be hoped that we shall receive invitations for the next garden party. I understand that His Highness means to have one every year from now on."

"You must have felt quite the hero, George," Lucy said, directing her gaze at Francis.

Francis shrugged. "I felt dashed foolish."

Lucy speared a piece of meat on to the end of her fork and with downcast eyes said demurely, "What a pity that *my* husband cannot boast such a mark of bravery."

Claudine threw her daughter-in-law a sharp look. "Francis's place is here at Frinton Park. The heir should never put himself at risk, much as he may desire to seek glory on the battlefield. He had a duty to remain at home with his family."

With a tremendous effort Lucy gathered up her courage, went very red in the face and blurted, "Then, ma'am, I regard it as a great misfortune that you did not think it necessary to teach your *eldest* son his duty. If you had he would not have gone off to the wars."

Claudine put down her knife and fork, stared for a moment at Lucy, then turned to her husband for guidance. Her look seemed to say, "Has she gone quite mad?"

James looked very taut and stiff, like a man who expects to receive a blow and has gathered himself up to counter it. Francis and George stared silently at their plates, casting covert glances at Lucy while they waited for her to reveal how much she knew. It proved to be a great deal more than they expected. It poured out in an accusing stream, starting with the cruel deception Francis and George had practised upon her—and upon their Mama added Lucy belatedly, with a glance at the stricken Claudine—going on to mention the terrible crimes committed by Sarah and George, with the latter not sticking at murder. She knew that those two had stolen things from many houses in the county, for she had seen and recognised certain pieces of jewellery, even a brooch of Mama's. Had Mama not noticed the loss? Thus appealed to, Claudine shook her head dumbly and Lucy rushed on, telling of Sarah's openly avowed intention to re-possess herself of the money and jewels which her father had confiscated.

It was more than Claudine's bemused brain could take in. Her hand flew to her head and she rose unsteadily to her feet, declaring feebly that she must go to her room . . . her head. James allowed her to go, regretting all the explaining he would have to do later. Claudine would pester him with questions until his own head swelled to the size of a football. In the end she would calm down and accept his assessment of the situation, along with his instructions as to their future handling of what was turning out to be a most complicated state of affairs.

Meanwhile, there was Lucy to be dealt with, firmly and authoritatively, a Lucy who was staring at him defiantly, challenging him to rebuke her. He would begin by endeavouring to placate, while trying to ignore the ghastly looks of his eldest son, who was vainly struggling to adapt to the fact that his brother and sister were not only deceivers, but thieves into the bargain, and that his brother, if Lucy was to be believed, was a murderer.

"So, Lucy," James said in his loudest and most aggressive manner, "you have somehow uncovered information which I had hoped to keep from you because I knew it would only cause you distress. You do understand that I knew nothing of my son's disgraceful behaviour until it was too late to undo the harm that had been done to you? You do understand that?" he repeated when she continued to regard him with sullen belligerence. His question produced a grudging affirmative and he went on, "So far as George and Sarah are concerned they will pay for their other misdemeanours by living good and useful lives from now on, exerting a strict form of self-discipline and a devotion to duty which George shall learn from me and Sarah from her husband."

"You call murder a misdemeanour, sir?" inquired Lucy, with an impudent sideways tilt of her head.

James's tightly compressed lips expressed his fury at having to knuckle under to the insolence of a young woman whose plain duty was to obey him. He said, "George has explained to my complete satisfaction the circumstances of that unfortunate incident. Your husband, ma'am, was being blackmailed by a whore with whom he had had a brief liaison before his marriage to you, and was provoked into doing what he did. You must believe me, my dear Lucy. I know a great deal more about the whole affair than you do, for the matter has been thoroughly thrashed out between myself and my two younger children." He finished sourly, "You should thank God that the mystery was never solved. Discovery would have brought disaster and disgrace upon our family."

James injected a note of sarcasm into his voice as he continued, "I do not know how you came by your dangerous knowledge, but would hazard a guess that you have been listening at key-holes. I shall not, however, presume to question you as to that. In return for my discretion I shall expect you to be similarly discreet, and uphold the honour of my . . . *your* family. The fact that you are married to George is surely irrelevant, since the marriage was arranged, and my eldest son's affections were not engaged."

The sheer arrogance of it astounded even Lucy who failed to see that James had his back up against the wall and was using every means, foul or fair, to extricate himself from an unsavoury mess. All she could think of was that she had greatly loved Francis and felt certain, had she been married to him instead of to George, that there would have been no estrangement between them. Even now, as she looked at Francis, her stomach turned over and her legs felt weak. She said, "As to my upholding the honour of the family, sir, I take you to mean that I must never speak of what I know, and I give you my solemn pledge that I shall not . . . provided that certain conditions which I shall make known to you are met."

James, who had begun to feel relieved by his daughter-in-law's opening words, quickly recognised that there was more to come. With an effort he kept his anger in check. "What conditions, Lucy?"

Lucy took a deep breath and plunged. "Dr. Pettit's partner, Dr. Webster, informed me a week ago that I am with child at last. I went to his consulting rooms in Brighton."

Little cries of astonishment greeted her news and George, who felt that his manhood had been vindicated, sat with a gratified smile on his face. Lucy ignored them all and went on imperturbably, "I am now quite resolved upon setting up my own establishment. It is to be separate from that of Mr George Darker, whom I no longer regard as my husband, but as a wicked imposter. The price of my discretion, Mr Darker, is a house of my own, fully furnished and staffed, where I may live in peace with my child. In other words, sir, in case I have not made it plain to you, I am demanding the return of my dowry on the grounds that it was handed over to you by my Papa on a false pretence."

All the time she was speaking James was regarding Lucy steadily, little Lucy with her longing to become a housewife, in possession of a set of keys to unlock every secret a house might hold for others, but must never hold for her. Lucy was putting him up for ransom in his own house. It was a distinctly unpleasant feeling. He said, with more composure than he felt, "And if I do not agree to your terms, my dear Lucy?"

The blue eyes of his daughter-in-law contained an icy

glint of determination which none of those present had ever seen there before. "Then, sir, I shall have no alternative but to take charge of the money and jewels which I came upon in the mausoleum and deliver them up to my great-uncle, Mr Justice Briggs-Watson, and I shall tell him where I found them . . . and what I chanced to overhear George and Sarah saying in the Morning Room . . . and how that Pinkerton woman came here posing as a milliner . . . and there will be an investigation."

There would indeed. James drew a long and heavy sigh and cursed the entire female population with their prying noses and their ever-alert, inquisitive ears. It was outrageous that two members of that wretched species should be openly defying his authority. It had come as quite a revelation to James to discover from the lips of Lucy that Sarah, far from being repentant after her experience in the mausoleum, was plotting further mischief. So she was determined to re-possess herself of the money and jewels was she? Not much chance of repentance there. Now here was Lucy demanding that he set her up in an establishment of her own to be paid for out of her dowry. Lucy did not know it, but her dowry, with George's consent, was going towards the considerable expenses which would be incurred when her father-in-law stood for Parliament. With an election coming up in six months' time James would need all the money he could raise.

James took an instant decision. Rising from the table, he directed a chilling look at Lucy and decreed, "You will remain in your bedroom, Lucy, until you experience a change of heart. I can only think that you have temporarily taken leave of your senses in making such an impudent demand upon me, and in daring to threaten me in my own house. You shall very soon become acquainted with the manner in which I deal with blackmailers. You shall not stir from your chamber until you see fit to return to me the property you have stolen from the mausoleum." His lips curled into a sneer. "I imagine that you have practised the usual female trick of hiding it somewhere else?"

Lucy did not answer. She was on her feet and would have run out of the Eating Room had not James thundered, "Stop her!" whereupon George, who had a great deal to lose if his wife should carry out her threat to expose him, was upon her in an instant, and at his father's direction bore her off upstairs to the accompaniment of screams and kicks, and a bite or two, which George repaid with hearty slaps as soon as he had set her down in their bedroom.

When the noise had subsided somewhat James pushed aside his plate, applied his napkin to his lips, and addressed his eldest son in stern and ringing tones. "You see now what you have brought about by your foolish prank? I hold you and George, and Sarah too, directly responsible for the turmoils which have rocked this house for the past two years."

Francis was looking deeply troubled. "I thought I had made it clear, Papa," answered he in a subdued voice, "just how much I regret ever having embarked upon such a hare-brained scheme."

"You had better have thought of it at the time," snapped James and abruptly left the room. In the hall he bumped into old William who wanted to know if Francis was taking a horse-whip to his wife. If so, declared the old man, it was not before time.

For the next four weeks Lucy remained a prisoner at Frinton Park, keeping to her locked bedroom when one of the family was not by to guard her. Her stubborn refusal to back down angered James beyond measure, and he personally conducted an inch by inch search of his house and grounds in an endeavour to uncover the place where Lucy had secreted the proceeds of the robberies.

Lucy gleefully hugged her secret to herself and spent her time reading Miss Austen's novels, thrilled by the exploits of Catherine Morland in "Northanger Abbey", and rather disappointed that the mysterious piece of paper, found by Miss Morland in a cupboard, had written upon it nothing more remarkable than a washing list.

Dr. Pettit visited Lucy on a routine call, with Claudine in attendance to make sure that her daughter-in-law held her tongue about the recent strange happenings at the Park. The physician thought his patient a little too thin and pale and advised regular exercise in the park and gardens. "But I am not per . . ." began Lucy craftily and was at once interrupted by Claudine, who smoothly inquired of the physician if there were any particular items of food from which Lucy would derive particular benefit in her condition. Successfully side-tracked, Dr. Pettit proceeded to name certain dairy products, and with a promise to call again in one month's time, was gone.

Lucy glared at her mother-in-law and picked up her novel. Behind this frail barrier she said defiantly, "You cannot keep me here for ever, you know. You may tell Mr Darker that I shall not waver from my resolution to be gone from this household and settled in my own abode. He has only to agree and I shall be no further trouble to him. Grandmama is sure to come to call soon, and she will want to see me. You will not be able to make sport with *her*."

This was very true reflected Claudine, who detested the situation which had arisen almost as much as Lucy. What Lucy did not know was that her grandmama had already called and had been put off by James, who had told her that Lucy was on a visit to her Peabody cousins at Horsham, and would not be back for at least six weeks. The old lady had gone away grumbling about the lack of consideration in young people these days. Madam Lucy should be taken to task for not letting her grandmama know beforehand that she intended to visit at Horsham. There were a great many messages from Sophie Briggs-Watson to be delivered in that quarter, and it was wickedly thoughtless of Lucy to go gallivanting off without consulting her grandmama. Unfortunately for Lucy she lived in an age when communication was neither swift nor reliable, and it was comparatively simple for people to indulge in a deception of this nature.

SEPTEMBER, 1815

Lucy sticks to her guns

Francis Darker, troubled by his father's words, and experiencing the beginnings of a mild distaste for the company of his brother and sister, whose recent misdeeds he so heartily deplored, went reluctantly to see Sarah and obtained from her, piece by piece, the whole sorry tale, starting from the time when Emily Pinkerton had put pressure on George to pay for her silence. He listened in growing dismay as Sarah elaborated upon the subterfuges practised by herself and George to steal the money and jewellery from Mr Darker's friends, not hesitating to rob their own relatives if the opportunity arose.

Sarah, her cheeks slightly flushed, spoke of how truly exciting it was to filch money literally from beneath the noses of unsuspecting victims, and afterwards to sit back and watch as the constables went round in circles desperately trying to lay the blame somewhere, anywhere, to save themselves from incurring the wrath of the gentry. "They even took up Annie Wilkinson," she giggled, naming the Lambton's parlour-maid, "until her lover came running down to Piddingfold gaol with proof, so *he* said, that she had spent the night of the robbery in question with him. What that proof was I have never been able to ascertain." Sarah giggled again, like a naughty child. "Perhaps Tom Perry showed the constables her nightshift."

"And are you not ashamed that you have caused so much havoc in the county?" Francis asked her curiously, his face sober as a judge's.

His sister pouted childishly. "It was extremely diverting until Papa found out about it and put a stop to it." Then, flinging herself against the back of the sofa she uttered the oft-repeated cry, "Oh, I do not know how I shall *endure* to go on living with Mr Cobbett. If only that fool of a Lucy had not interfered I should have discovered for myself that Papa had left the money in the mausoleum. Piddingfold would not have seen my face again." Her hands went up to claw at her hair. "I have been so *stupid*! I should have *guessed* that Papa would leave the money where it was."

"Are you so unhappy here then?"

"Wretchedly so," she confessed at once and burst into tears. She covered her face with her hands and sobbed aloud, parting her fingers to peer at him mournfully. "Shall not you hate to stay here, knowing that you will never now be able to resume your rightful place as father's heir?"

"I shall endeavour to get used to it," he answered, and knew that he would never get used to it, not if he lived to be a hundred. He remembered how he had longed to see Frinton Park again, even as he fought on the field of Waterloo and rated his chances of survival as less than fifty-fifty.

She was quick to notice his shifting glance, and dropping her hands sat up straight, squaring her shoulders. "I should not care to be cheated out of *my* rights." Carefully she watched his reaction to these words. "I should make it quite plain to Papa that I had no intention of being deprived of my inheritance."

He smiled ruefully. "I am in no position at present to demand anything from Papa."

There was a lengthy pause, during which Sarah tried to read her brother's mind. After a while she said, "If either you or I could persuade Lucy to reveal the whereabouts of the money and jewels we could be off to London together, or wherever you pleased, Francis, and we would have enough to buy a fine house, where you would be the master and I the mistress, until you should choose to marry." Sarah's eyes shone as she resurrected the old, worn-out dream, substituting Francis for George because the latter had lost his appetite for rebellion. "I could take Thomas and pay a lawyer to obtain an annulment of my marriage, and next time I should be mighty careful to choose a husband who knows how to treat a lady, one who can afford to buy me fine clothes and jewels, and keep up a handsome carriage."

He wondered what grounds she would fabricate in order to obtain an annulment of a marriage which had borne fruit, and even as he formulated the thought he guessed that the child, his nephew, was the son of the vanished Captain Millars. He asked quietly, "What of George?"

She shrugged, an uncaring little lift of the shoulders which made him sad. "George will be content to stay here, and Lucy will settle down when her baby is born. Motherhood has a marvellously quietening effect upon a woman."

He argued with the ghost of a smile, "Not in your case."

At this she laughed quite gaily. "I freely admit that I do not feel the same maternal instincts as most women of my acquaintance, but I should not care to abandon my son to the tender mercies of a village school-master, who will bring him up with ideas far below his station." Her eyes pleaded for understanding. "Oh, Francis, we could be so happy living together, you and I, away from Mama and Papa and my beast of a spouse. All three try to make me do things for which I have no stomach. They will not allow me to be *free.*" She slid off the sofa and came to kneel before her brother, taking his hands in hers. "Please, Francis. There is nothing for you here in Piddingfold. You are a man of the world now and should look to make yourself a fortune. You cannot do that if you are for ever shackled to Papa and dependent upon the paltry allowance he will pay you."

Her words found melancholy echoes in his heart, for

since his return from France, longing for home and eager to make reparation for the wrong he had done his family, he had been made all too well aware that the price of forgiveness would come high. His father had spoken of his hopes for the future and of how he, Francis, who must now accept his role as the younger son, would be expected to lend his aid to the Jamaican enterprise and perhaps remain for long months, even permanently, on the opposite side of the world. He had hoped so much that he might once more become Francis Darker, and now it seemed that he must be content to play the role of George for the rest of his days, accepting the inferior benefits of a younger son—unless he could find the means to change his father's mind.

George, he knew, would make a better sugar-planter than he. He had realised, alas too late, just what Frinton Park had meant to him and what a crass idiot he had been to give it all up. Having acquired a greater degree of maturity as a result of his recent experiences he had realised something else too. In time he could have grown fond of pretty Lucy, and marriage to her would not have seemed half so bad as he had at first anticipated, for she had truly loved him. Deceived by George, perhaps she had dimly perceived that something was wrong, without being able to say what it was, and she had masked her unease under harsh words and petty bickering. But it was too late now to have romantic thoughts about Lucy. He looked into his sister's wide, anxious eyes and withdrawing his hands from hers said, "I shall need time to think about it."

"Yes, yes, all the time in the world, dear Francis," she agreed eagerly, and would have said more had not Mr Cobbett, tired out and hot from his labours with the young, come into the parlour and, with a frankly admiring nod, acknowledged the presence of his brother-in-law.

"Ah, George, how very pleasant to see you. Shall you stay for tea?" and as Francis was about to declare that he had a number of things to do, "But you must, my dear fellow, for I am not quite clear upon a point which I raised with you on the last occasion we met. Did the 1st and 3rd Grenadiers really put to rout Bonaparte's famous Imperial Guard, and what was the final outcome of that particular engagement? How many of our brave fellows were left dead on the field?"

Mr Cobbett had at last found one member of the Darker family whom he could "take to" and from whom he could derive an excitingly vicarious pleasure as he listened to a succession of war reminiscences. This young hero of Waterloo could provide all the dreams of glory Mr Cobbett had ever yearned for.

Francis knocked on Lucy's bedroom door and went in at her invitation. Her face tightened into a look of prim defensiveness as she saw who had disturbed her reading, but she laid her book down and looked up at him inquiringly, hoping very much that he had not come to badger her like the others. Hardly half a day was allowed to pass before they came to wheedle and hector, persuade and bully by turns. She had held out for five long weeks now and was beginning to lose hope of ever regaining her freedom, watched as she was day and night. She now felt that if only she could break loose and run from the house she would be content merely to fall into the arms of her doting grandmama and be happy to forget all that had gone before.

Several times she had been sorely tempted to give in, but those insistent Darker faces, with their constantly changing expressions, now frowning, now placating, now dangerously angry, made her keep to her resolve to carry on with her plan which had gone so badly awry. She longed for Dr. Pettit to come again—he was due in two weeks' time—so that she might secretly pass him a note, slipping it perhaps into his little black bag when she was sure of remaining unobserved. The note would instruct Dr. Pettit to tell her grandmama that she was being forcibly held at Frinton Park, and to please to come at once and rescue her. She was certain that such a ruse would be successful, and then these horrid Darkers would be made to pay very dearly for their abominable treatment of her. Grandmama, though once a Darker herself, would see to that.

It seemed to Lucy that she would never now obtain a home of her own, but she did not really care any more. All she wanted to do was to get away. Meanwhile, as long as she refused to tell any of them where she had hidden the stolen property they would not harm her. Lucy wondered uneasily why the idea that one of the Darkers might offer her bodily harm had come into her head at all. That was indeed a ridiculous notion and must be dismissed at once.

She waited for Francis to speak, and when he did so was surprised by the gentleness of his tone. He was the only one so far who had not pestered her, but she felt sure that *they* had sent him as a last resort, in the hope that he might be able to persuade her to reveal her secret. If they thought that they were in for a surprise. With a hesitant, almost timid smile, Francis pulled a chair round to face her and sat down, engaging her glance with such an earnest look that she was forced to turn her head away.

"Lucy, my dearest Lucy, how greatly I have wronged you."

She knew it was a trap to lull her into a false sense of security. Oh dear, why was she suddenly filled with the most urgent desire to burst into tears? She became quite alarmed when he rose suddenly and came to sit beside her on the green and silver striped sofa. His blue eyes were full of sincerity as he went on, "I have come to beg your forgiveness for the terrible injury I have wrought upon a sweet and innocent lady."

At that moment she could not have trusted herself to speak, so large was the lump in her throat. He took her hand and gently insisted, "Can you forgive me, dearest Lucy?"

She shook her head, still unable to speak. "Ah." He gave

a despairing little sigh. "I thought the offence had been too great."

"*They* sent you," she accused at last in a small, choked voice. "Papa and George and Sarah. They want you to make me tell you where I have hidden the money."

"No, no." He shook his head several times. "Lucy, my very dear Lucy, I am a returned soldier who is tired of war, and wants only to settle down quietly and earn his bread as a simple farmer. I greatly deplore what Papa is doing to you, and can only hope that he will come to his senses and return your dowry, so that you may attain your heart's desire and buy a house of your own."

His shoulders heaved regretfully. "Would that I might share it with you, for I believe now that I love you. But for my folly, my only excuse for which is that we were *commanded* to love each other, when the more sensible way would have been to allow nature to take its course, we could be man and wife together now, and the child you carry would be my son or daughter."

This pretty sentiment brought on a fresh flood of tears and a muffled, "I love you too, Francis. I have done so from the very first." A reproachful upward look prompted him to respond wistfully, "What a villain I have been."

"Is it not possible . . . ?" she began and finished with a rush, "for us to be together?"

He looked at her longingly. "Oh, dear heart, would that it were!" Her eyes flared wide with hope before her mouth drooped, and tears oozed from under her lashes to run down her cheeks. "Papa will keep me here for ever. He will never give in and return my dowry." A whining note had crept into Lucy's voice, reminiscent of the tone she had used in the frequent exchanges she had had with her husband.

"We could use the money you took from the mausoleum."

She stared at him with a frightened expression. "Stolen money?"

He looked very serious as he answered, "It is regrettable, to say the least, that the money can never be returned to its rightful owners. I suppose that Papa might have meant to keep it in the mausoleum for ever, perhaps to be used by generations of Darkers as yet unborn. Even stolen money achieves a certain degree of respectability over the years."

"It is not fair!" Lucy was red with indignation.

Francis laughed softly. "Nothing is ever fair in this world, my dear Lucy."

She got up from her chair and began pacing agitatedly up and down, wringing her hands. "It would not be right, Francis." It was a statement, made with vehemence, to convince herself.

He was at her side in an instant. "Your own house, Lucy, in which you may come and go as you please, and where the ordering of the servants will be in your hands alone. You will not even have to change your name, and I swear that I shall do everything in my power to make you truly happy. We could live in Hampshire, perhaps, and Great-Aunt Sophie could come and visit us whenever she pleased." She was gazing at him now with the transfixed air of a rabbit before a poised predator. "Tel me where you have hidden the money, Lucy."

She came out of her trance to hit him hard across the cheek. "Papa and the others, they *did* send you!"

He nursed his smarting cheek and managed to make his eyes look hurt and defeated. "Oh, heavens!" She hid her face in her hands. "You are driving me insane, all of you. You will murder my unborn child between you."

He said soberly, "I have offered you my heart, Lucy, and would offer you my hand if that were possible. Please believe that I shall always keep faith with you." With that he was gone, leaving her in a state of wretched indecision.

Francis reported a third failure.

"I should like to wring her stupid neck!" exclaimed Sarah. "That silly creature!"

Her brother was merely amused by such extravagances of expression. "Patience," he counselled. "I shall prevail upon her yet. You may be sure of it."

"I hope so," snapped Sarah.

Francis spoke further reassuring words and prepared himself for yet another verbal onslaught upon the beleaguered Lucy.

Lucy, work-bag and novel in hand, walked through the park to the summer-house. There she intended to spend the morning quietly immersed in "Mansfield Park", her reading interspersed with half-an-hour or so of embroidery. She had obtained this unusual concession by virtue of the fact that her husband and father-in-law had gone to Lewes for the purpose of collecting from the bank the Michaelmas wages of all the servants and tenants on the Frinton Park estate. Claudine, backed up by Francis, had agreed that she might take the air as far as the summer-house, putting her upon oath not to stray further. With her now habitual sad expression Claudine had emphasized that it would be the undoing of both herself and Francis if Mr Darker were to discover that his orders had been disobeyed. "Lucy dear," she had pleaded, her dark eyes mournful, "do not you think it is time that you gave in, if only for the sake of your child? You require so much more exercise than you are presently accustomed to take, and you are completely cut off from society. It cannot be good for you."

Lucy, who liked Claudine better now that she too had become the victim of the tyrannical behaviour of James Darker, very much wanted to give in and return the stolen property to her father-in-law, but the stubborn streak, inherited from her maternal grandmother, was always strong enough to pull her up short as soon as she experienced the onset of weakness. She had therefore dropped her eyes before Claudine's beseeching look, and without another word had fled to the safety of the summer-house.

Mrs Sarah Cobbett, toiling up the carriage-drive on a morning visit to her mother, caught sight of the ripening figure flitting across the lawn without the customary chaperonage of a member of the family. She was immediately on the alert, and casting about her to see that she was not observed, she cut across the lawn in the direction of the summer-house, plainly her sister-in-law's destination. When she arrived, a trifle breathless, at the aforesaid building, a rectangular brick and wrought-iron structure built by William Darker in the days when such things were the height of architectural fashion, she came upon Lucy comfortably ensconced in one of the cane chairs, a cushion tucked into the small of her back, a novel on her lap and her work-bag at her feet.

Lucy looked up with a start as Sarah entered and seemed to recoil, pressing herself against the back of her chair and gripping the arm-rests with tightly curled fingers. The other's voice was sharp and imperious. "Did Papa give you leave to come here alone?"

Knowing it was fruitless to lie, for the relentless Sarah would search out the truth later anyway, Lucy shook her head. "But Mama said that I might come here, and so did Francis. I gave my solemn word to Mama not to stir until it is time to go in for dinner."

"And they believed that you would honour such a pledge?" sneered Sarah dropping into a chair.

Lucy bridled. "Why should they not?"

Sarah blinked rapidly several times, but made no reply to this challenge. The two women sat, their eyes locked, with Lucy hoping very much that Sarah would not stay long and spoil her entire morning. She looked so very hard and unbending sitting there and attempting to stare her out of countenance.

"Well, Lucy," pursued Sarah briskly, "so you are determined to keep your little secret locked fast in your bosom? That is very brave of you, my dear, but do not think for one moment that Papa will give in and buy you your house, or, for that matter, that he will return your dowry. I, for one, have never heard of such a ridiculous fancy. You have a perfectly good home here with George, and should be content that your child will always be well cared and provided for."

Lucy had an answer to that one. "And I suppose that you are content, Sarah, with Mr Cobbett, and would not dream of ever running away and setting up on your own? It seems to me that you are in no position to cast the first stone. Indeed, you should have a great deal of sympathy with me, for you are in much the same situation. Neither of us is very much attached to our husbands."

Sarah frowned, fidgeted with her gloves, and answered crossly, "Our cases are quite different. I was forced, through adverse circumstances, to marry beneath me, whereas you have a husband who is your equal in society. It appears to me that you choose not to make the best of your marriage."

"*I* was deceived!" retorted Lucy hotly, "and for that I have to thank you and your brothers, who like to play foolish and dangerous games."

"Francis did not love you," came the cruel rejoinder. "He was only too pleased to exchange the prospect of sharing your soft bed for a hard straw pallet in a tent in Portugal. You should think yourself lucky that George, who was so much attached to you, was willing to engage in a deception merely to have the pleasure of your company for the rest of his life. If a man did that for me I should count myself thrice blessed. You had not the sense to benefit from your good fortune, but must make George's life a perfect misery with your whining complaints."

Lucy bit her lip and murmured, "You will never understand, any of you, how much I have been wronged." Fiercely she attacked Sarah. "Do not think that you will be able to keep me a prisoner here for very much longer.

Already Dr. Pettit thinks it mighty strange that I do not get about more in society. He was quite sure that I should be at the Lambton's At Home last month, and remarked upon the fact that I was not . . . and my grandmama is bound to come visiting soon."

That made Sarah laugh. "Great-Aunt Sophie thinks that you are away visiting your cousins at Horsham and will not be returning for several weeks, so she will not be poking her long nose into our affairs just yet."

At this Lucy gave a little wailing cry and burst into tears. "I hate you! I hate all of you! I shall tell my grandmama. . . ."

She gave vent to a frightened shriek as Sarah leapt forward from her chair and pounced on her, clasping her round the neck and shaking her savagely back and forth. "You *shall* tell me. I shall *make* you tell me," she threatened. "You little fool. Do you not see that Papa will kill you before he allows you to dishonour the good name of our family? *Now tell me!*" This last, furiously shrieked injunction, was accompanied by a gradual tightening of her fingers about Lucy's throat.

Lucy's eyes rolled back into her head, and her hands came up to claw at Sarah's fingers. Sarah, all self-control fast disappearing into the whirlpool of blind frustration, continued to exert pressure on her neck and Lucy's vision became blurred by bright flashing circles of light and little coloured dots which came and went. Her sister-in-law, incited to a killing rage by the suffering of weeks of anxiety as she waited for Lucy to weaken in her resolve to remain silent, was within an ace of committing murder when a harsh masculine voice thundered, *"That is enough!"*

Francis plucked his sister away from Lucy and shook her like a rag doll. "That is not the way!" he hissed into her ear, and pushed her out of the summer-house with a low-voiced instruction to go up to the house. Then he turned his attention to the wilting Lucy, who lay back in her chair with one hand clutching at her throat and making small gasping noises. Francis gathered her up in his arms and hugged her to him. "My poor child," he murmured. "My poor, poor child. They shall not use you so. I shall put an end to this charade as soon as father returns from Lewes. He must allow you to go where you will, and he shall return at least some of your money. I shall insist that he does, and in this I know that I shall have Mama on my side."

She was sobbing wildly now and clinging to him as though her life depended on it. Through her sobs she managed to gasp out, "Take me away . . . please take me away, Francis. I cannot bear it, truly I cannot . . . I cannot, oh, please. . . ."

He sat down in the chair and took her on his knee, rocking her to and fro as if dealing with a distressed child. After a while she calmed down, but he could not detach her hand from her throat. "Does it hurt much?" he inquired solicitously.

"Very much," she whispered.

"Poor little bird." He kissed the side of her neck and she produced a very shaky smile. Her hand fell away from her neck at last and he could see the beginnings of the small purple bruises left by Sarah's cruel fingers. They shocked him more than many of the awful sights he had seen while he had been fighting abroad. They were proof of a savage intent to kill for personal gain. Like George before her Sarah would not stick at murder to get what she wanted. They were bad seed, both of them, and he wanted nothing more to do with their nasty little intrigues.

Meanwhile, there was Lucy to be soothed and cajoled, and lied to just a little until he could determine upon a sensible course of action. Already an ominous quivering of the lips betokened the onset of a fresh bout of tears. Lucy was still in a state bordering on shock. She swallowed hard. "Shall you take me away today, Francis?"

"Not today, dear Lucy," said he gently. "You must go back to the house and be very patient for a little while." He took her hands in his. "Trust me," he said. "There shall be no more unhappiness for you from now on."

Lucy ran so hard that she got a stitch in her side. Home, where Mama, Papa and Grandmama lived, was still half a mile away. She could see the house spread out upon the crown of the hill, a gracious Elizabethan mansion enclosed in a protective ring of oaks.

It was almost two miles from Frinton Park to Southwood Place and it was not good for the baby, she knew, to run like this, especially as she was crying all the time, which made her progress somewhat erratic and very breathless. Hampered as she was by the ubiquitous work-bag, that commonplace article which no one at the Park had suspected as being the key to her well-kept secret, Lucy had covered the distance at a speed which she would not have believed possible, spurred on by misery and by a burning desire to pour out her troubles into the sympathetic ears waiting for her on the hill.

The full majesty of the law

Mr Justice Briggs-Watson, sunk deep into his leather armchair, and with his wig awry, peered at his dead brother's wife over the top of his square-rimmed spectacles, refusing absolutely to be put off by the baleful glare directed at him. "If, ma'am," said he sternly, "you consider it an impertinence on my part to attempt to get at the truth of this extraordinary affair, then I am heartily sorry for it. If I offend by. . . ."

Sophie Briggs-Watson's black-mittened hand waved him to silence with ill-concealed impatience. She had known Timothy Briggs-Watson since they were children together, and was not inclined to take it seriously when the old lawyer climbed upon his high horse.

"My dear Timothy, I merely wish to impress upon you that my grand-daughter is not given to telling falsehoods, neither is she inclined to take a fit of the vapours without good cause. You may believe that what she tells you is the exact truth and nothing but the truth." The grim little mouth perked up into a sly grin. "Is not that the jargon you lawyers use in court?"

Lucy, observing the two elderly sparring partners from the seclusion of her chair by the open window wished only that she might lie down with a wet cloth on her forehead and a few drops of laudanum inside her to soothe away the throb in her temples. She had told them all she knew. Why did they not get on and do something about it? Lucy was ignorant of the fact that the law is a ponderous machine, and that it would be many days before the necessary questions and answers had all been given.

Meanwhile, Mr Justice Briggs-Watson, having expressed his doubts, and having received a resounding rebuke for his pains, thought it high time to delve deeper into the matter. "Well now," said he, drumming his fingers on the arms of his chair, "What do we have? Three young persons concoct a mischievous plan to deceive their elders. One of those young persons goes off to war, leaving the other two behind to play a dangerous little game of their own which does not stop at murder.

"Even if I accept that everything Lucy has told me is correct down to the smallest detail, I must still ask myself, Where is the proof? Should I dare to proceed upon a tale overheard by a third party behind the curtains of a window-seat I should be laughed out of countenance, and the production of property which is known to be stolen will not suffice to point the finger of suspicion in any particular direction. A vagrant thief could have left the spoils of robbery in the Frinton Park mausoleum."

Timothy Briggs-Watson lifted his thick shoulders in order to emphasize his point and stared challengingly at Aunt Sophie. The old lady returned the searching look with interest, her sharp blue eyes unflinching before the solemn gaze of magisterial dignity. "I can give you proof." She hesitated briefly. "At least . . . I can put you in the way of obtaining it."

White, bushy eyebrows rose inquiringly, and Aunt Sophie's steely resolution faltered momentarily as she contemplated what she was about to do. What a scandal she would bring down upon the heads of her brother and his family! What a cause célèbre she was about to set in motion! She had always been a hard, vindictive woman. One of the great pleasures of her life had been the enjoyment she derived from observing at a distance the misfortunes of others, but she had looked after her own, strictly adhering to that golden, inflexible rule that the family must stick together at all costs, in order to ward off any threat from outsiders.

Until now. Now, the one person Sophie had truly and unselfishly loved had been cruelly tricked, and used to further the ends of that trio of scheming rascals up at the Park. Sophie bit her lip with yellowing, aged teeth, flecked with brown spots of decay, and pulled herself together for the final, determined onslaught. She repeated firmly, "I can put you in the way of obtaining it."

The white eyebrows rose even higher, an abrasive, almost mocking gesture to spur her on. She said: "George has a large round mole on his hind-quarters. There is your proof of identity. The man who now poses as Francis Darker is in reality his brother George, as you will very soon discover when you arrest him."

Aunt Sophie's glance strayed briefly and came to rest on Lucy, drooping by the window, and Timothy Briggs-Watson sensed the inward struggle taking place beneath that withered bosom, saw the unaccustomed tenderness in the still alert eyes, absorbed through his very pores the old woman's feelings of outrage. He thought he detected an effort to hold back tears as she faced him once more and declared, "A wicked deception has been perpetrated, and my grand-daughter was married under false pretences to an imposter."

The magistrate's face folded into a light, reproving smile. "It would appear, ma'am, that you attach greater importance to the charge of deception than to that of murder."

"So I do!" she snapped. "I shall never forgive my nephews for what they have done, though I'd lay wager that it was Sarah who was the instigator of the whole miserable business."

The magistrate stretched out his hand towards the glass of madeira which glowed invitingly on the table beside his chair, prompting Sophie to take up her glass also. The two offered each other a silent toast and sipped at the rich, full-bodied liquid respectfully. Timothy Briggs-Watson ran a large pink tongue round secretive lawyer's lips. "So," he said, "we have a charge of deception, capable of proof, which can be laid against Francis and George Darker. I can certainly issue a warrant for their apprehension on those grounds and perhaps, under intensive interrogation, other, more serious matters, will come to light."

"There is no doubt in my mind," Aunt Sophie said positively, "that the mysterious thieves who have been abroad in this neighbourhood for the last few months are none other than George and Sarah. James and Claudine know what they have been up to. It all came out when James discovered the pair of them in the mausoleum, although Claudine did not learn the truth until my poor little sweetheart tried her pathetic attempt at blackmail."

Another darting look was directed at Lucy, but the girl did not respond. She sat bow-backed by the window, her eyes idly following the antics of two of her grandmother's labradors who were romping on the lawn. Sophie gave up the attempt to engage her grand-daughter's attention and continued her tirade. "That Mrs Barrett, Claudine's sewing woman. She knows something. She was there when James spun his tale to the servants about George and Sarah having been set upon by robbers. She has a nose for a mystery, that woman. When she last came here to sew for me her tongue was on the wag the whole time."

Aunt Sophie mimicked the pseudo-genteel tones of the sempstress. " 'Does it not seem strange to you, ma'am, that a thief should have chosen the Park as a repository for his ill-gotten gains? Is it not possible that one of the servants who is not honest has some villainous outside connection? They are saying in the village that Mr Darker took on a new stable-boy without a character. Should not that be looked into, ma'am?' . . . and so on, until she made my head ache.

"To tell the truth, I paid little heed to what the garrulous creature was saying. Wish I had now, but all is not lost. I can send for her again and draw her out. She'll not need much encouragement." Sophie sucked in her cheeks and looked pensive before adding darkly, "It will not take me long to break Claudine down. She'd never the stomach to stand up to me."

Mr Justice Briggs-Watson began to feel warm under his wig. He made as if to remove this irritating encumbrance, but remembered in the nick of time that it was impossible to do so in front of ladies. "Let us assume then," said he, "that we have a reasonable chance of bringing a charge of theft against these young offenders. That still leaves the charge of murder, and if you will take my advice, ma'am, you will make no effort to uncover any facts concerning that unfortunate affair. It has long been forgotten in the county. I can understand that you have an earnest desire to see your grand-daughter avenged for the wrong that has been done to her, but I cannot believe that it is your wish to prod one of your great-nephews in the direction of the gallows."

He wagged a stubby forefinger at her. "For such would be the outcome if George were to be found guilty on the greater charge. If the lesser charge of robbery is proved, both George Darker and his sister would set sail for Botany

Bay, and you would not see them more for at least seven years."

Sophie's decaying teeth dealt with a Bath biscuit. She swallowed another sip of madeira to wash it down. As she did so her mind went back many years to the time when her own brother had been revealed as the murderer of a black slave who had been brought to England from the West Indian islands on one of her brother William's ships. There were still a few people in Piddingfold who remembered that dreadful business and its sordid aftermath. What would they say to a second scandal in the Darker family?

Sophie was about to concede that deception and theft would do when Lucy rose suddenly from her chair and came to stand directly in front of her great-uncle. The intensity of her gaze as she met his eye disturbed him not a little, and he stiffened, as if preparing to repel a threat, the nature of which he was not yet able to determine.

"No," Lucy said in a low voice, "he shall not get away with murder. He shall pay for what he has done to me and to that poor girl . . . whore though she was."

At the same time as his eyes took in the pretty, flushed face, the resentful eyes and trembling mouth Timothy Briggs-Watson's lawyer's brain registered the fact that his niece gave herself precedence over the murdered woman in the matter of injury sustained. The phrase "a woman scorned" flitted through his mind, and even as it did so Lucy leant a little towards him and enunciated very clearly two words, "*The watch*."

"The watch?" he repeated, and sat up straighter in his chair, fighting off a vague sense of premonition. Aunt Sophie paused in the act of raising the glass of madeira to her lips and sat as if turned to stone.

Lucy's voice was quietly venomous. "It said in the "Brighton Courier" at the time of the murder of Emily Pinkerton that the constables found a watch in the burnt-out room and that it must have belonged to the murderer, because the man who was with Miss Pinkerton had a watch in his waistcoat pocket, and it was therefore not likely that the second watch belonged to him too. What has become of that other watch?"

Her uncle, shaken to the very foundations of his soul, returned gravely, "As material evidence of murder the watch would have been retained. It will be in the courthouse at Lewes. No doubt it will have been blackened by the fire which broke out in the room where Miss Pinkerton died."

"But it will still be recognisable?"

"Indeed, yes."

"Then send for that watch, Uncle," implored Lucy, "and I will identify it for you as having once belonged to the man I married."

"You seem very sure, my dear," he murmured despairingly.

She straightened and moved away from him, her hand outstretched to toy with a pair of white and gold Staffordshire china dogs which adorned a side table. Picking up one of the dogs she traced a line of glazed gold with her forefinger. "I *am* sure, Uncle Briggs-Watson." She sounded detached, almost as if she had lost interest in the subject under discussion. "When George and Francis changed places they took care to change clothes and possessions too, but George could not bear to part with his watch because Francis's watch is not near so fine, and George has a weakness for expensive jewellery. He therefore kept the watch and put it about that "George" had given it to him as a parting gift and keepsake before going off to the wars."

The china dog was being inspected in all its parts, Lucy's finger outlining its ears as she concluded relentlessly, "I believe that George lost his watch at the time Emily Pinkerton was murdered. I remember remarking that he never seemed to wear it any more."

The magistrate gave a long, shuddering sigh, as one

accepting defeat, and asked, "Is the watch plainly identifiable? Many gentlemen own pocket watches of a similar appearance."

Lucy replaced the dog on the table and took up its fellow, repeating the same rather eerie process of inspection. "The watch is gold and has a small knob at the side near the winder. The knob forms part of the decoration surrounding the dial and cannot immediately be perceived by the casual observer. When pressed, the knob activates a spring and the back flies open. Engraved inside are the words, "To George Darker, my beloved grandson, from Elizabeth Branson"." Lucy turned to face her grandmother. "You have seen the watch opened, Grandmama, have you not?"

Sophie nodded briefly and downed the rest of her madeira at a single gulp. Mr Justice Briggs-Watson heaved himself up out of the depths of his chair. Six feet of bone and muscle towered over Lucy and her grandmother. Addressing his next remark more particularly to the latter he said loudly, "If I proceed with this matter it will cause a stir such as the county has never before seen, and it will bring James Darker to his knees."

Aunt Sophie's hand trembled slightly as she replaced her empty glass on the table, but Lucy's voice came out strong and clear. "If you do not, sir, the stir will be the greater, since I shall accuse you of withholding evidence which might convict a murderer."

Mr Justice Briggs-Watson's legs collapsed under him. The chair received his weight with a loud protest of springs.

NOVEMBER, 1815

Trial by Jury

The arrest and subsequent trial at Lewes Assizes of George Darker and Sarah Cobbett caused such a commotion in the county that it was reported in the London newspapers, and people flocked into Lewes from as far afield as Kent and Surrey in order to witness the judicial proceedings.

The charge of deception against Francis Darker was dropped for lack of evidence, for who could say, with hand on heart, that it was not he who had stood up in Piddingfold church beside Lucy Briggs-Watson, and that the brothers had not changed places on the very day of the nuptials *after* the ceremony had taken place? Who could now untangle the ravelled web of contradictions which the young people at Frinton Park had woven?

No witnesses from the great houses in the county came forward to testify against George and Sarah in connection with the recent spate of robberies, even though, in the light of certain revelations, suspicions in various quarters must have been mounting, and many a two and two now put together totalled four. One drew one's own conclusions, but one did not betray one's own kind.

As far as the servants were concerned, however, the rule of ancient loyalties did not apply, and some of those who had been dismissed under a cloud, after having been wrongly accused of stealing, clambered eagerly up the well-worn oaken steps of the witness-box to give their evidence in halting, rustic tones, declaring under oath that they had actually seen Master George and Miss Sarah . . . "er, the prisoners, my Lord . . . entering the Master Bedroom furtive-like, when the rest of the company was engaged in conversation below-stairs in the saloon."

Annie Wilkinson, one of the maids from Glynwood Manor, the home of Mr George Lambton, went even further. Addressing the bench, her apple cheeks riper than usual with the excitement of the occasion, she stated boldly, "I saw 'em both, sir, coming up the back stairs, and whispering together, and laughing like, and then Mr Darker says quite loud, 'Stand by the door, Sarah and don't you let no one come in till I'm done!' "

Mr Justice Carter's marble-cold eyes bore down upon the witness with alarming severity. "And you reported nothing of this to your mistress at the time the incident took place?"

Annie stared up at the magistrate and tucked an errant curl into her white cotton cap with one trembling finger. "She wouldn't have believed me, sir. 'Tis not for the likes of me to speak out against the gentry. I'll lose my place as 'tis. . . ." and in a final outburst of defiance, "but 'tisn't right they should get away with it and innocent folks be took up for what they 'aven't done. . . ."

"Yes, yes, that is *enough*!" Mr Justice Carter frowned Annie to silence and for once found himself at a loss for words.

Other servants stepped into the witness-box, gradually building up the case against George and Sarah until there was not a single soul in the courtroom that was not convinced of their guilt.

As to the charge of murder against George Darker, lumped in with the rest, as was the fashion in early nineteenth-century England, here an unexpected witness came forward in the person of Madame Renée, the Brighton milliner, at whose sought-after establishment in East Street Emily Pinkerton had once been employed.

Madame Renée, attired in an embroidered gown of white muslin, mulberry velvet spencer, and a pink silk turban topped with ostrich feathers, stepped daintily into the witness-box, removed her pink mittens with the air of one having all the time in the world, propped her parasol against the rail and took the oath in low, genteel tones. She was a tall, buxom brunette with pink cheeks, aided by art, and active black eyes which took in the details of her surroundings with the speed of an ant-eater darting for its prey. Conscious of her importance as a witness she devoured Prosecuting Counsel with a glance of such palpitating intensity that a gentleman less wise in the ways of the world, and of women in particular, might have been quite overcome. As it was, the case-hardened attorney thought of her only as his prize witness and was determined to make the most of her, leading her with consummate skill towards the administration of the coup de grâce.

Slack-mouthed and sullen in the dock George Darker listened with growing dismay to Madame Renée's evidence, in which Emily Pinkerton's sudden acquisition of the sum of £3,500 with which to set up in business on her own account figured large.

Prosecuting Counsel probed deeper. "Did Miss Pinkerton say where this rather substantial sum had been acquired?"

"She said she obtained it from one of her gentlemen friends."

Prosecuting Counsel: "Rather a large sum for a gentleman to give to a part-time whore, was it not?"

Madame Renée (bridling): "I did not inquire into the exact circumstances. I. . . ."

Prosecuting Counsel (cutting smoothly across attempted speculation): "Did it not cross your mind, ma'am, that the deceased might have been stooping to blackmail one of her . . . er, clients? Whores have a distressing propensity for tricks of this nature I believe."

(Objecting, Defending Counsel protested that Prosecuting Counsel was leading the witness and inviting her to indulge in flights of fancy.)

Overruled.

Mr Justice Carter: "You will please to answer the question, ma'am."

Madame Renée (hesitating): "Well, she did say that those who played dirty deserved to be made to pay."

A rising crescendo of laughter in the courtroom died grudgingly away as Mr Justice Carter's gavel thundered a tattoo on the bench.

The questioning went on, with Madame Renée growing more and more flushed by the minute, and in the end hotly defending herself for not reporting her suspicions to the authorities, even when she heard that Emily Pinkerton had been murdered in her own "palace of pleasure."

The satin bows, the feathers and the lace ruffles were all wilting dismally as the milliner climbed down from the witness-box and took her place on the witnesses' bench amidst a bombardment of boos and catcalls. When the hubbub subsided Prosecuting Counsel rose to announce, with an air of unmistakable triumph, that his case was concluded. Let Defending Counsel extricate his clients if he could!

James Darker entered the "White Hart" inn by a side door and was conducted by the discreet and sympathetic landlord to an upper room where his friend, Lord Frederick Oliver waited to take lunch with him. The deafening noise from the tap-room, muted by plaster and wood, rumbled monotonously under their feet as they sat down at table.

James's face was a drawn white mask of pain and bewilderment. Fred could hardly bear to look at him, and to cover his embarrassment snatched up a flagon of port, which he had had the foresight to order beforehand, and poured James a full glass. The other took it with a silent nod of thanks and drained it at a single swallow, wiping his mouth with the back of one hand, and with the other placing the empty glass upside down on the table in the manner of one toasting the corpse at a funeral. Fred, meanwhile, rang the bell and ordered a servant to bring up lunch, taking it upon himself to choose James's food for him, in order to give the distraught man time to regain a measure of composure.

A full ten minutes elapsed before Fred ventured to speak. "I stayed until eleven o'clock when that milliner woman was giving evidence. I must say, dear fellow, that things look pretty bad."

James propped an elbow on the table and massaged his chin, his fingers exploring the stubble of two days' growth. "It is bad," he agreed flatly. "They will find my son and daughter guilty. The one will hang and the other will be transported."

Fred had known James too long to attempt a false and comforting denial. Before he could formulate any sort of reply at all the latter had crashed his clenched fist down on to the table, causing the flagon and glasses to tremble. "*Why did she do it?*"

Fred had already been regaled with the whole sorry tale of Lucy's attempt at blackmail and her subsequent flight from Frinton Park. "Lucy? I suppose she had a compulsive urge for her wrongs to be redressed."

James poured himself another glass of port and drank it down. "I under-estimated our little mouse. She has become a veritable tigress in her desire for revenge."

Fred toyed with the flagon of port, his hands as restless as those of his friend. "I would never have believed," said he, "that a prank played by three mischievous young persons could have resulted in a tragedy of such monstrous proportions."

"It will ruin me," opined James. "Parliament must do without me, and as for making contacts with a view to reviving my business interests, I shall henceforth be astonished if any man should venture to shake me by the hand, or show the smallest gesture of goodwill towards me. I shall never live down the disgrace, and my son and daughter have gone beyond the point where I can feel the least pity for their plight."

In some distress at his friend's outspokenness Fred changed the subject. As their meal was brought up and served he inquired, "How is Claudine?"

James contemplated his mutton chops with gloomy distaste. "Shut in her bedroom and refusing to speak to anyone. She has withdrawn into a private world of her own and rebuffs all attempts to pull her out of it. If she does not rouse herself soon I fear she will go mad."

Fred speared a potato. "What a very convenient solution. How clever of Claudine to have thought of it."

James pushed his plate aside. "You never really took to Claudine, did you, Fred?"

Fred made no direct reply to this question, merely observing mildly, "Follies of our youth, dear fellow. Dalliance on the Grand Tour turning into tragedy for me and a lifetime of regrets for you."

James, steadily drinking himself into incoherence, mumbled, "Both had our troubles . . . you and me, Fred. Dodgson will be avenged when they sentence Sarah . . . give you some satisfaction."

"No satisfaction whatsoever, dear fellow," returned Fred quietly. "What's done is done."

James applied himself once more to the port. "Youth of today . . . no stamina . . . no discipline . . . gone to the bad . . . a rope, and a ship to Botany Bay. . . ."

"You still have Francis," Fred reminded him.

James struggled up through the gathering fog of inebriation. "I shall never forgive him for ducking out of his responsibilites in order to go soldiering. He is as much to blame as the other two."

Fred picked at his meal in silence for a while, watching sadly while his friend sank deeper and deeper into a wine-induced stupor of self-pity. Long before James fell sideways to the floor Fred had reached the conclusion that, distasteful as it would be to him, he must go across the road to the court-house and hear the verdicts delivered upon two young people he had known since birth.

Guilty as Charged

The verdicts, as the saying goes, were a foregone conclusion, and the sentences as easily predictable, except that Sarah received twelve years' transportation instead of the expected seven, a tribute to the disgust she had engendered in the stony breast of Mr Justice Carter.

At Frinton Park the servants went about their duties in stunned silence; Claudine sat in her room working on a piece of tapestry, her eyes never wavering from the coloured silks which ran through her fingers; James idled in the library with a bottle of brandy and his own private, bitter thoughts; and old William Darker visited the offices of Braithwaite and Braithwaite in Lewes, there to make certain changes in his will.

Safe at the house of her grandmother, Lucy felt her child stir within her and knew that she must bring forth the son of a murderer. Now that revenge for all her wrongs was about to be exacted in full a strange sort of lassitude had descended upon Lucy, and she no longer felt any exultation or even satisfaction that justice had been done. She would soon be made a widow, and it was unlikely that anyone, ever again would express a desire to marry her.

Francis went to see his brother in the condemned cell at Lewes gaol and was shocked by the other's appearance. George had become much thinner, and his clothes hung on him with the shapeless disinterest of cast-offs. He looked like the scarecrows scattered about the wheat fields at Frinton Park.

The prisoner lay stretched out on the mean truckle-bed provided for him, his eyes directed at the ceiling in a fixed, glazed stare. It was as if he sought to see beyond the grimy stone to a brighter, more hopeful vision. He did not move as Francis, stooping to avoid knocking his head on the door-lintel, entered the foetid hole and lowered himself upon the solitary stool, taking care to avert his eyes from the lidless bucket in the corner.

"They might have provided you with a table," he complained, looking about him with eyes which flinched from every detail. "There must be letters you wish to write."

George's head turned slightly, and for the first time Francis saw the blue eyes starting from the thin, pinched face, the mouth down-turned in stubborn rebellion against his fate.

"To whom?"

The words, uttered in a low, sombre tone, bore witness to utter despair. Francis leaned forward, resting elbows on knees, trying unsuccessfully to remain at ease in the taut atmosphere of terror which emanated from his brother. "To Mama, perhaps," he suggested.

"So that she may throw a fit of hysterics and run away to her bedroom complaining of a headache?"

"To Papa then. A word of contrition might comfort him."

With a suddenness which took Francis completely by surprise, George sat bolt upright on the bed and pointed an accusing finger. "Contrite is it? Have you forgotten, brother, that it was *I* who was against the business of impersonation right from the start . . . all those months ago when we three gathered in the Morning Room like guilty conspirators and plotted our own downfall? That it was *I* who sounded the single note of caution, and you and Sarah who would have none of it, but must force me into taking part in your accursed practical joke? It was *you* who hinted that Lucy would be miserable if she were married to you. What irony, eh?" he continued relentlessly. "Lucy could not have been more miserable had she been married to Satan himself, and it was all your doing, yours and

Sarah's. You led me by the nose down the path to *perdition!*"

George's voice had risen higher and higher as he made this speech, and small flecks of white appeared at the corners of his mouth. Francis was appalled. He had come to console, and to take a dignified farewell of his brother, and had not been prepared for the bitterness and hatred which washed over him in a hysterical tide of abuse. Francis, the soldier, did not fear death. He had taken part in the most terrible battle of all, in a field near Waterloo, and had seen the cannon balls cutting their way through the ranks of the men like knives through butter, leaving in their wake a tangled mess of flesh, blood and bone; he had bayoneted a French grenadier at close quarters and had held a dying comrade in his arms. He had seen into the pit of hell. In the arid plains of Spain and Portugal and the green fields of France and Belgium he had tasted both joy and exquisite terror, and death, his constant companion, had seemed a little thing. Perhaps he had known no worse grief than he experienced at this present moment as he gazed upon his mirror-image and recognised a coward.

There was a tremulous, womanish whine in George's voice as he raked over the ashes of the past and moaned, "If only we had not changed places. If only I had taken up the commission intended for me. I might have died like a man then. If only you had not persuaded me . . . been less insistent . . . if only. . . ." Near hysteria had given way to useless reminiscence which went on and on.

When Francis could stand it no longer he interrupted with, "I have permission to visit Sarah. Have you a message for her?"

A glint of malice in the pale blue eyes and the embittered mouth flicking up into a grin. "The same message she will have for you, brother. Go to hell."

"I am told that she is repentant."

"Hah!" George's bark of laughter was brief and unmirthful. "While it suits her she is. While it *hurts*. Take away the sting and she'll not be so docile."

Francis said soberly, "I doubt if she will survive it . . . being transported I mean . . . so it is questionable, George, whether her fate be better or worse than yours."

"She will survive," came the sharp rejoinder. "She will set her cap at some gullible farmer or factory owner who buys her for a slave, and in no time at all their situations will become reversed. The master will become the slave and the slave the mistress . . . in more ways than one."

There seemed to be nothing more to say, and Francis began to wonder how he should terminate this melancholy interview. He no longer hoped for a manly yet tender leave-taking, and regretted that he must depart without his brother having expressed any sentiments which might give him comfort in the years to come. It was truly wretched to part thus, and he would have given much for it to be otherwise.

George flopped back on to the bed and resumed his perusal of the ceiling, presenting a pathetic-looking figure in his soiled shirt and green, knee-length breeches. A strip of black silk adhered to his right cheek, covering a cut left by the careless prison barber, and his hair had been cropped short. Francis had brought clean linen for his brother, but he had been forced to hand these articles over to the gaoler lest some means by which the prisoner could cheat the hangman were concealed within the folds of a garment.

Hesitantly he rose to his feet. "I have left clean linen with the gaoler. . . ." He leaned over the inert form and offered his hand. "Come now, George, let us at least shake hands." To his surprise, Francis's hand was taken and firmly squeezed. Expressionless eyes stared up at him.

When the gaoler came in to tell Francis that his time was up the visitor was already waiting by the door, his chin buried in the collar of his redingcote as he prepared to meet the biting November wind. The man glanced at the bed, shrugged his shoulders and commented, "Face to the wall. Won't talk to no one since the judge passed sentence." He sounded aggrieved as he went on, "Meself, I like them as goes cheerful to the gallows. Being a gentleman I should'a thought he would'a done, but you never can tell."

He shrugged again, regarding the visitor with a knowing smile. "A crown would make it easier for your brother, sir. Good nip o' rum mixed with a drop or two of laudanum before he walks out. That way 'is legs'll turn to jelly and his head'll be so full o' wool that he won't hardly know nothing about it."

An eager hand was already outstretched before the silver crown was brought to light, and dirty fingers closed lovingly round it, like some deadly sea anenome caging its prey. The figure on the bed moved not a muscle as the door clanged shut behind his brother and the gaoler.

William takes a hand

William Darker removed his new percussion-cap pistol from its velvet-lined case and laid it carefully on the table before him. The sun, slanting through the square-paned windows of his bedroom, lighted upon the deadly weapon and turned it into a thing of beauty. William handled the pistol reverently, running his fingers over the polished walnut stock, tracing the outline of his own name engraved on a silver label above the words "Smith of London," twisting the "scent-bottle" powder container, testing the mechanism of the striking pin which protruded from one end.

It was not long, however, before he gave up this contemplative pursuit and became on a sudden brisk and business-like. He laid the pistol on the table and unscrewed the little cylindrical box of percussion caps. With facile economy of movement he extracted one of the round plugs and inserted it into the breech of the pistol, rotated the magazine to release a small quantity of powder which dropped on to the plug, and locked the hammer into place.

After satisfying himself that he had loaded the weapon correctly William placed it in the pocket of his flared coat and with purposeful steps quitted the bedroom, descended the long, curving staircase, and directed his feet towards the Morning Room. The door of that chamber stood slightly ajar, and through the aperture thus formed William could see his grandson seated upon the sofa and thumbing through an illustrated catalogue. The name "Forsyth," glimpsed on the back cover of the catalogue, would have told William, if he had not known already, that the young man was interested in guns.

A grim smile, not untinged with sadness, played about the old man's lips as he pushed open the door, removed the pistol from his pocket, and before his grandson had time to look up, shot him through the heart. The pistol discharged with a noise loud enough to dislodge the starlings from a nearby chestnut tree, and William just had time to thrust the smoking weapon into the dead man's limp hand and make his exit through the window before James Darker came crashing into the Morning Room.

Upstairs in her bedroom Claudine too heard the sound, raised her eyes momentarily from her work and lowered them again with an expression compounded of puzzlement and pained disapproval. Loud explosions were distracting, but they had nothing to do with her.

Sophie Briggs-Watson sat facing her brother in her private sitting-room at Southwood Place and mumbled crossly through a piece of toffee, "I shall not go to any more funerals . . . except my own that is. They remind me too much that my time is nearly up. Morbid things, funerals. . . . What will James do now that he has no heir? Adopt that brat of Sarah's?" She poked a forefinger into her mouth in an effort to detach the sticky brown substance from the back of one of her front teeth, and having succeeded, continued more intelligibly, "I never thought Francis would be so lacking in spirit that he would take his own life. He was always my favourite, you know. Thought he had more guts than George. He could ride a horse like the Devil himself."

Her thin, reedy cackle grated on William's nerves. He remembered the old days when the high, malicious laugh of a young girl had had the same effect upon him.

Sophie grumbled on. "If I had known he was going for a soldier instead of George I would have given him the Palomino. Might have guessed really. . . . Francis would have joined a cavalry regiment. . . . He should not have taken his own life. . . ."

All at once William lost patience with senile garrulity. "He did not take his own life. I killed him."

Sophie stopped chewing and sat bolt upright in her chair. "*You* . . . killed Francis?"

"No," returned William calmly, "I killed George."

For the first time in her life Sophie felt a little faint. She clutched the arms of her chair to steady herself and took several deep breaths. After a while a little colour flowed back into her cheeks. "For God's sake, William," she whispered. "What are you saying?"

As was usual for him in moments of tension William had recourse to his pipe, and removing this comfortable article from his pocket, together with his tobacco pouch, began the long process of filling and lighting it. "They did it again, you see," he observed casually, avoiding his sister's eye. His plump, red features screwed themselves into a knot of concentration as he crumbled a plug of tobacco between his fingers.

"Who did what?" inquired Sophie huskily. She was still not in command of herself.

"George and Francis. They changed places again."

Sophie's hands fluttered together and were clasped tightly against her narrow breast. "Lord preserve us, then it was Francis they. . . ."

". . . hanged. Yes, it was Francis," William finished for her.

Sophie was quite out of her depth. "Why did Francis let them. . . ? How did George. . . ? she floundered, and then losing all patience, "For heavens' sake, William, what is this all *about?*"

"Stop rattling and I will tell you." William tamped down the tobacco in his pipe with a practised forefinger. There was a kind of sly triumph in the hard grey eyes which looked across the room at his sister. "I knew the first time. I knew they had changed places and that Francis had gone off to the wars leaving George at home."

Sophie's unswerving stare held a wealth of indignation. "Then why in heavens' name did you not say so at the time? You would have saved everyone a deal of misery."

Her brother countered equably, "At the *time* I did not think it mattered a jot which one of James's boys inherited Frinton Park. They were both born on the same day, when all is said and done, and if the eldest by a few minutes had a yearning to go soldiering, let him I thought. The other will do well enough at home."

"And what of Lucy?" demanded Sophie hotly. Did you not think of her? The poor child became prey to a most monstrous deception, and she truly loved Francis."

William, who had never believed in the existence of love between a man and a woman dismissed this argument with an indifferent shrug. "I reckoned she would breed the same from George as she would from Francis, and I have been proved right, even if it did take her longer than most."

Sophie ignored this masculine logic and demanded, "*How* did you know?"

For answer William gestured at her inquiringly with his

pipe which produced an immediate and impatient, "Oh, for God's sake, William, light the foul thing. I wonder you even bother to ask my permission . . . and do *get on*. How did you know that George and Francis had changed places?"

"Because," said William, "Francis came to see me the night before he went away to join his regiment, to take his leave of me, you understand. I gave him twenty guineas as a parting gift. 'I promise not to spend it on loose women or drink, Grandpapa,' said he, and I could see that he was a thought overwhelmed, because he had not expected anything better than a handshake and my good wishes.

"He started to fiddle with his hair, taking up a strand between his fingers and twisting it round and round, and as we stood there staring at each other like a couple of fools, neither of us knowing how to make the break, it flashed through my mind that never had I ever seen George mess about with his hair like that. It was Francis who played with his hair, a habit he had inherited from my Clarissa, God rest her, and it was Francis who now stood before me."

William broke off to light his pipe, taking so long to ignite the wax taper at the fire that Sophie thought she would scream. When at last the lighted taper was applied to the tobacco Sophie recoiled slightly as her nostrils rebelled against the acrid smell of smoke. If he noticed his sister's discomfiture William chose to ignore it. He had never had much time for Sophie. It was only now that the two of them were in their dotage that they had come closer together, drawn to each other perhaps by a common sadness at the passing of the old, rumbustious days of their youth, when they had fought each other tooth and nail upon every subject under the sun.

William essayed a few experimental puffs to make sure that his pipe was alight then leaned back in his chair to resume his tale. "Realisation of the truth must have shown plain upon my face, because Francis stepped back a pace or two, as though he feared I might strike him, then said very low, 'Shall you tell on us, Grandpapa?'

"I was so shaken by what had happened that I could not for the moment speak. The boy fell on his knees before me and with tears in his eyes poured out a torrent of words to the effect that he had always wanted to be soldier, and that he could not abide young Lucy, and had no desire to marry her."

A tightening of Sophie's lips was her only reaction to this piece of heresy. William continued, "I could not bear to see the lad weep, though I knew him to be no less a man for it, and I gave my promise that his father and mother should know nothing from me." The old man hesitated a bit before admitting, "If I had stopped to think the matter over more deeply I daresay I should have come to a different conclusion altogether. I should have known there would be trouble over it sooner or later."

"So you should!" snapped Sophie. "You kept quiet all those months while the mischief was brewing!"

William went on the defensive. "How in God's name was I to know what George and Sarah were up to? They had leave to come and go without my say-so. Thought me a poor, doddering old fool I shouldn't wonder, though they were not too proud to prod me into telling them tales about the slave-trade when they'd nothing better to do." He gave a short, neighing laugh.

"What then?" prompted Sophie sharply. "You kept quiet, I suppose, when you heard that Lucy had set the cat amongst the pigeons by trying to bludgeon James into returning her dowry?"

Her brother nodded emphatically. "Least said, soonest mended, I thought."

"And you thought wrong, did you not?" retorted his sister sarcastically, "because the thing pretty soon got out of hand, with Sarah frightening Lucy half out of her wits by trying to choke the truth out of her."

"And you putting the lid on the pot by running with your tales to old Tim Briggs-Watson."

It was Sophie's turn to go on the defensive. She said sulkily, "I had no alternative. Lucy was bent upon bringing George to justice. I was much against her delving into the business of murder, but she would have her way. Nothing I could say would have stopped her."

"Maybe not," mused William.

A long period of silence ensued, during which William puffed out wreaths of smoke and Sophie struggled with her reluctance to face the fact that Francis, the once loved great-nephew, had been hanged in the mistaken belief that he was George. William, not usually very perceptive with regard to the feelings of others, seemed on this occasion to sense Sophie's desire to shy from the truth and said quietly, "You may take my word for it that the man who was hanged at Lewes was Francis, and that he whom I shot was George. Do you want to know the manner in which it came about?"

Her face twisted into a grimace which reminded him of the sixteen-year-old Sophie being made to do something against her will. At length she confessed. "I must know all."

"Very well then. I expect you are aware that Francis went to Lewes gaol to take his leave of George on the night before the execution. Somehow, and that I can only guess at, for I am hardly in a position to question the gaoler and arouse even the glimmer of a suspicion, I believe George overpowered his brother, changed clothes with him, and left him stunned in his cell. Then he walked out of gaol a free man. He probably left Francis lying on the bed and persuaded the gaoler that his brother was too grief-stricken to speak."

Sophie was bursting with questions. They died at birth in the face of William's impatiently waving pipe-stem. "You can fill in the details for yourself," he said. "When George came back to Frinton Park he went straight to

Francis's room and stayed there. James and I took supper alone together that night, and that poor creature Claudine remained as usual in her bedroom.

"The following morning I was the only one who had the stomach to go to Lewes and witness the execution. I did it because I thought it was my duty to do so. It was only fitting that George should not be left to die without a single Darker there to see him make an end. When they brought him out I forced my way to the front of the crowd. His back was to me when the chaplain was praying, and then the hangman turned him about, placed the rope about his neck and bent to pick up that black bag they put over their heads. I remember noticing a long scar on the side of his face and thinking how strange it was that he should have scratched himself in the identical place where his brother bore a mark.

"In that instant his eyes met mine and he said, very clear, 'I spent the twenty guineas on a saddle, Grandpapa.' For a moment I was so stunned that I could not move, and then my arms were waving in all directions and I was bawling at the top of my lungs, "No, no! You are hanging the wrong man!" The people who knew me thought I was demented with grief, and I was borne to the ground by a dozen hands as I struggled to climb up on to the scaffold."

A tear oozed its way out of William's eye and rolled down his cheek. "They meant well, those miserable fools, plying me with brandy and offering their condolences on the fate of my grandson, but by the time I had struggled to my feet it was all over, and Francis had departed this world. I know not how I returned home. My horse found its own way. All I could think of was that George must not be allowed to get away with murder a second time, and it seemed the easiest and most fitting thing to take the matter into my own hands and be my grandson's executioner."

For Sophie, the depths of human experience had been plumbed. Shock and grief gave way to fatalistic acceptance of a mischief which could not be undone. She asked dully,

"Was James so blind that he could not see what was plainly apparent to you?"

William gave a grunt which might have expressed anything from contempt to simple amusement. "James's world came crashing about his ears when George was convicted as a murderer, and the prospect of his own future advancement faded into obscurity. He noticed nothing, not even the fact that "Francis" had covered the scar on his face with a black patch. Nice touch that, wasn't it? I wonder how long George thought he could get away with it? Probably intended to take off for foreign parts . . ." William pulled up short and steered the conversation round to more immediate matters. He said with a frown, "James worries me. He is still going about his daily round like a man in a trance. Next thing you know he will take to the bottle and that will be the end of him."

"And of Frinton Park," Sophie said. "The place will fall into decay long before Lucy's child is old enough to hold it together."

"Maybe not," William said thoughtfully. "James has not yet inherited Frinton Park, and will not do so while I am above ground. Perhaps Lord Frederick Oliver can be persuaded to hold the estate in trust after my death for the next generation. Upon one matter I am quite determined. What I have built up shall not be destroyed by my son's over-indulgence in the bottle."

"Do you remember," said Sophie, "when Cousin Patience. . . ."

"Do not speak of that!" he ordered her peremptorily. "If it had not been for Cousin Patience none of the rest would have followed. James would not have married Claudine, and I might have enjoyed a peaceful old age, without memories of a trio of devil-spawned brats who trod the path to hell." He added with some of his old fervour, "God grant me enough years to set it all to rights."

"Amen to that," said Sophie.